I0548052

"You must sign register!"

I ease on back into the dojang. What register? Black belt etiquette is new. What's the deal? Mistress Kim explains: "Register, you sign. All blacka belts, this recorded on roster in Korea from here. Unnerstand?"

Sure, of course, this tells the people who invented the art who is involved and how involved they've become.

I'm stunned to see next to my name "black American."

It's easy to understand the urge to codify—a no designation at all means "white," of course, and "Bi Bim Bap" means Korean, of course, but "black American," nawww, that ain't me.

Sorry, Miss Kim, I can't sign this."

"Blacka belt register, you sign!" Clearly a hint of future problems to come between the African-American communities and mono-culturalized Koreans.

"I'll have to talk with your husband about this."

I handed the belt (quivering, beautiful, my name in gold thread) back to her. She vehemently refused it— "No, yours. Master this evening." He was "*the* Master"; she called him "Master."

I walked home from the dojang feeling confused and a little bit disgusted.

by Odie Hawkins

Brazilian Nights
Black Chicago
The Busting Out of an Ordinary Man
The Life and Times of Chester L. Simmons
Chicago Hustle
Chester L. Simmons AKA The Great Lawd Buddha
Menfriends
Portrait of Simone
Ghetto Sketches
Conspiracy
Scars and Memories
Secret Music
Sweet Peter Deeder
Memoirs of a Black Casanova
Amazing Grace and Other States of Mind
Lost Angeles

LOST ANGELES

ODIE HAWKINS

Originally published by Folio Graphics Co., Inc.

Copyright © 1994, 2011 by Odie Hawkins

Front cover photo by Zola Salena-Hawkins,
www.flickr.com/photos/32886903@N02

ISBN: 978-1-5040-3587-3

Distributed in 2016 by Open Road Distribution
180 Maiden Lane
New York, NY 10038
www.openroadmedia.com

LOST ANGELES

It was 1971 and here is a sampling of what was happening:

Israeli-Arab peace talks resume. President Nixon cites congressional failures, covers wide range of issues in T.V. interview. House ruling hailed, speedier criminal trials ordered. Military shake up in Bolivia. Cuba's "Year of Productivity." Swiss court approves giving bank data.

British envoy kidnapped in Uruguay. North Vietnam missile base hit; other Indochina developments. Supreme Court backs welfare visits, denies Hoffa petition, accepts Ali's draft appeal. Haitian hints son to be successor.

British doctors condemn smoking. Bethlehem Steel charged with job bias. Nebraska #1 in final AP poll. *New York Times* begins publishing secret Pentagon papers until temporarily halted by court order; covert war policy indicated.

Oil prices increased in Nigeria. Terrorist attacks in

Northern Ireland. Land mine kills South African police. U.S.–Japan sign pact on return of Okinawa. World Court rebukes South Africa on her administration in Namibia.

House passes welfare reform bill. Consumer prices rise again; personal income, housing starts rise. Gains for Neo-Fascists in Italy; police crackdown on Mafia. Mexico City mayor quits after disorders.

Kissinger to Saigon for talks. In Middle East, Jerusalem Arabs to be compensated, Israelis invade Lebanon, Jordan begins commando purge. Black Muslims. Supreme Court accepts Ali appeal, reverses Ali conviction.

Fourteen Chicago lawmen indicted in Hampton case. Theater—*Black Terror: A Black guerrilla revolution in America*. Written by Richard Wesley. Directed by Nathan George. Produced by N.Y. Shakespeare Festival. With Kain and Don Blakely.

Chapter 1

An interesting number gets played out these days by fifty-year-old brothers who've had white women play prominent roles in their lives; some of them go into a deep denial mode. It's impossible to clarify their motivations. Some of them go the opposite route and claim to be victorious warriors because they rode their masters' "mares" to victory. Etc., etc., etc.,...

A few admit to "jungle fever," circa '60s, plus psychological-standup-tragedy feelings. Fewer still will admit, "I have no fucking idea in the world how we got together, based on where she was comin' from and where I had been."

Marlene and I come closest to the "no-fuckin'-idea-in-this-world-how-we-got-together" syndrome than any of the other vibes. I'll give in to any contrary theories whatsoever.

It started meaning more to me as time went on, after we

had "divorced," than it ever meant when we were together. It hadn't been "jungle fever" in New York, Chicago, Philly, or even "El-A," for that matter. How do they get the nerve?

No, this was a different vibe. This woman who was smart enough to whisper secret shit in six languages had finally agreed (after a summer of jive letters—mine) to return to Compton to be with me.

I was—how do you say?—floored! I couldn't believe that this major league Euro-American (white? whose white?) woman was willing to come back from Kissinger's Washington to share Compton's realities with me. I was touched.

"This war is being fought for the dope trade, the dope coming out of Laos, Cambodia, and Vietnam. It might be America's opium war."

"Oh yeahhh," I nodded. What else could I do? What else had the government told me to do? Incidents, of course, began to change public opinion considerably.

I liked Marlene from the beginning. I had no choice. She was a stunningly attractive woman filled with good vibes and ingenuity, but she was white/European, and that bugged the fuck out of me for a long time. (Don't listen to those African-American men who say, "Uhhh, well, I don't really pay any attention to Franique's racial background. She's just a human being to me....")

I thought about us *not* getting together and finally conceded that it would be better for us *to* get together, more for my daughter's welfare than mine. I was coming away from a doomed marriage with a child from another marriage, more doomed than the last one. We pulled it together in an L-shaped room in Compton. It would be damned near impossible to recap the vibes that allowed us to believe that we could make it out of the L-shaped room. But we

10

were Believers; I discovered that she had an intact belief system right away.

"You can write. Write. I'll get a job, and your writing will become famous, and you'll become rich and support me."

It almost happened like that, almost. Stuff did begin to happen with her help. I retrieved my daughter from my ex-wife (the family becomes extended with each marriage), and we moved to a larger apartment in Compton. The only martial art I was practicing at the time was survival. I had gotten a job as a laborer in the Stauffer Chemical Company in South Gate.

Vicious place to work. Vicious. They were manufacturing tripolyphosphate (whatever the fuck that is); there wasn't a sack in the place that weighed under fifty pounds; and the place was filled with rednecks, stoic Gros Ventre Native Americans (one of them told me that a Stauffer man had wandered onto their reservation and recruited), a weird collection of second generation Mexican Americans who often stood around telling "wetback" jokes, and four other brothers.

We worked rotating shifts, which meant it was impossible to develop a regular sleep pattern. Just when you had adjusted your metabolism to the 8:00 AM to 4:30 PM shift, it was time to get on the swing shift. And finally midnights. It was a mean scene. Everything in the place was dangerous: wires here that could decapitate, vats full of bubbling shit, hundred-pound sacks of stuff piled in pyramids (they were apt to topple over on you if you tried to write a poem in their shadow), and occasionally, depending on how evil the rednecks felt, someone might fling a brick or wrench down on you.

It paid to wear your helmet even during the lunch break.

I was writing lots of poems and attending as many writ-

11

ing workshops as possible. Marlene was reinforcing my creative drive every step of the way. The conflict of being a Stauffer slave and a creative being was forcing me to do a lot of weird stuff. I had to decide whether or not I was going to eat lunch or write a poem or try to get thirty minutes' sleep. It wouldn't seem to be a big thing, but it was.

I was saved from the horrors of the place by a phone call. During the course of one of my days off I had applied for a job as a "community service trainee" with the Concentrated Employment Program. Counselor Pat Falls, bless her sweet heart, called me in the sulfite warehouse to give me the good news.

"You can start next Monday, if you like."

I was so happy I almost cried. A "community service trainee." I was in heaven. The pay was a fourth less than I was making as a Stauffer slave, but I would be able to write on the job. I resigned that afternoon and began to prepare myself to become the best "community service trainee" the Concentrated Employment Program had ever had.

The idea behind the "community service trainee" bit was fairly radical. There were thirteen of us, and our job description included "relating to the community." Specifically, I ran around to people's houses who had job appointments, to jar them out of lethargy, to prod them into offices to fill out applications. On more than one occasion I had to take prospective employees to thrift shops for a decent set of clothes. I was good at my job and I was writing.

I was in the Watts Writers Workshop and we were hot and getting hotter. You could tell by the ink that was given us in the *Los Angeles Times*.

"Watts Writers Workshop, Budd Schulberg, blah, blah, blah...." It wasn't Schulberg for me; it was a guy named Bloch, who led writing workshops that were precisely that, a new concept at the time. A lot of post-Watts Rebellion

12

people thought that the writing workshops were supposed to be group therapy sessions, ways and means to blow off steam.

Louise Meriwether, John Bloch, and a couple of other hip teachers wouldn't buy into the post-outrage bullshit; they were into the craft of writing, and if you weren't, then Too Bad. It was a really strange time; there was everything and nothing. People were being given contracts for bullshit and people were being given contracts for non-bullshit.

Bloch became a patron. After having me write a few short stories for a couple of years ("to get them right"), he took me by the hand to Robinson and Weintraub, agents. I was making enough money to retire my friend from "active duty." We were moving on; it was Happening.

The house we rented on 17th Street (right off Arlington) was the peak point of the year. I had a screenplay (commissioned by Cinemation Industries) to write, a few residuals coming in, a woman who loved me at home, and a trio of lovers on the side. What more could I ask for?

Hapkido was calling. Maybe the need to have a martial art was prompted by dealing with Hollywood's crazy shit.

Chapter 2

My mind wanders—89, 90, 91, 92, 93—am I counting to one hundred or two hundred!? 94, 95, 96—it must be one hundred. It would have to be one hundred. He wouldn't make me do two hundred, would he?

One hundred sidekicks with the left leg; now change to do one hundred with the right leg. I lowered my leg to the concrete surrounding the canvas mat, my left leg deadened from the terrible pain of kicking at a distant point, the ball joint in my hip screaming.

"Mah!"

Master Jun Bai Lee growls at me, his face hidden by the pages of the *Korea Times*. I am made to understand, once again, that he reads my intentions and will not permit me to take it easy, to focus on my pain.

I have no idea what "mah!" means, but it seems to convey the worst kind of promise. If you don't continue to do the kicks, I'll make you do something harder.

15

"Mah!"

If you persist in thinking about fluffing off, I'll come over there and pinch a nerve that will electrify you with pain.

"Mah!"

The right leg lifts itself, chambers, fires off a bullet kick; the Master lowers his newspaper and says in his heavy Korean accent, "Good kick; ninety-nine more, all same."

2, 3, 4, 5, 6, 7, 8, 9, 10, 11, 12, 13, 14....

Before and after class I have a few moments to look around, think about what I'm doing. For the first time in my life I'm not punching a clock. I'm writing novels and screenplays, I'm being paid nice money to do what I love. The hapkido dojang (studio) is a grim place. Master Lee has converted a deserted storefront into a hapkido academy. He has burrowed into a dimly lit space, fenced off a section of the interior with a low wooden bannister, and covered the wooden ribs in the floor with flattened Kleenex boxes and a canvas mat that burns the skin each time you slide away from a flip or throw. Those awful ribs in the floor are the things to watch out for. Hapkido involves a lot of flips and being thrown to the mat, and the thing to do is make sure you land between the valleys of the ribs. To be thrown across the ribs may fracture one of your own ribs.

Check out meat being grilled to appreciate this subtle distinction.

I was Master Lee's number one and only student for months. It didn't take a genius to understand why. The physical environment was quite depressing and the master was from the old school.

I shuffled off to class (four blocks from home), praying that some other mad person had joined me, someone to share the pain with. No such luck.

Well, to be truthful, a few strays wandered in from time to time, stayed for a demo class, and left immediately thereafter.

Mondays, Wednesdays, Fridays, and sometimes Saturdays. I used to go to class sometimes thinking, will this man treat me as badly today as he treated me last time? He never disappointed me.

Master Jun Bai Lee was an incredible looking person, first: a kind of elfin Korean at four-foot-ten or so. He was a thirty-year-old-man who had learned his hapkido from monks in the mountains of South Korea. It was obvious that he had suffered a lot (the flattened bridge of his nose, the leg wrappings on the right knee, the bitter strength in his sparkling brown eyes) and that he was not going to soften/modify his art for western students.

The sauce was served at one level—hot—and you had to take it or leave it. It would be hard to say, at this point, if I would've accepted his invitation to learn hapkido if I had had any inkling of what I was going to be dealing with.

"Suffering" is the only word in English that analogizes hapkido training, if done properly. And Master Lee was about the business of doing it to you properly. During those crazy moments when the lights went out in my head and I felt as though one of my legs had dropped off, or that my left elbow had been reversed, I thought about dropping out, not paying dues for the next month, fleeing to the safety of the nearest lounge. I couldn't do it because I was afraid of what would happen to me. That's how deeply he had gotten to me.

"Mah!"

I spent equally perplexing moments asking myself three questions: What the hell am I doing in this place? What am I doing? How did I get here?

The last question was easier to answer than the first two.

Hapkido called me; I hadn't asked for it: it was literally that simple.

Why was I strolling west on Pico (near 4th Street) one afternoon, on the north side of the street, a few blocks from home? What was I doing? Who knows? Maybe just sniffing around for foreign piss stains, taking a break from the joys of screenplay writing—circa 1971.

The finger that looked like a crooked nail curled, gestured for me to come inside. Something about that finger should've been a tipoff that I was about to be pulled into something beyond me. I cautiously stepped into the dojang he had converted from a mom 'n pop store. He explained to me that I needed a white dobok (white workout clothes), thirty dollars, and that I should be in class promptly at 4:30 PM the following day.

It would be impossible to record how I was made to understand any of this because Master Lee's English language skills were sub-rudimentary. But somehow it was clear: I was going to be Master Jun Bai Lee's first student.

The tortures began on the first day and never ceased. Strange hurts: the back of the left heel, the third rib on the left side, a serious tingling in both elbows, a crick in the neck—some days the whole body. I had no idea what hapkido was, really, or what you were supposed to do in it. Superficially I knew it involved punching and kicking. It was, after all, an Asian martial art; and they were all involved with kicking and punching, weren't they?

There was no section of my head that was reserved for anything Korean. I was beginning to love Thai curries and Japanese sushi, but those were purely restaurant concerns, nothing holistic. I knew where Korea (both of them) was from studying the geography book, but I knew zip about Koreans, their culture, language, history, music, art, prejudices, religious practices, stereotypes, attitudes, hapkido.

I learned quickly.

90, 91, 92, 93, 94, 95, 96, 97, 98, 99, 100. My right leg now feels as dead as my left leg. In a way, they both feel like the same leg. I have no way of knowing how to take the first step after the ball bearings in both my hip sockets have been burned out. That's the feeling.

The Master carefully folds his newspaper, snorts through his deviated septum, and gestures for me to join him on the mat. Somehow I manage to take the few steps onto the mat, where he begins to teach me a series of punishing, pain-loaded holds and throws.

I want to ask him if these boa constrictor clinches and monkey tosses have names, but the pain is too intense, there is no time. I'm either spanking the mat with pain or I'm flying over his shoulder onto an unribbed section of the floor (I pray). Did he understand that I was an African-American person, with specific historical books? Did he relate to my incredible heritage? Did he care about me?

Years later, when the Korean-merchant/African-American-liquor-store wars commenced, I felt I had a secret handle on something. I paid my dues and prayed that others would join me, share the torture, fantasizing that their presence would leaven the punishment....

"Mah!"

They trickled in toward the end of the first year. I cursed them in my sleep. Where were they when I needed them? Master awarded me the red belt after a cold-blooded series of tests. He smiled at me and clapped me on the back. After a year of brutalizing me he smiled at me. I was too frightened to smile back. He grabbed me by the scruff of my neck and force-fed me through six belt levels (white, yellow, blue, green, brown, red) in a traumatic year. I wasn't ecstatic. I was humbled.

He had crushed my head in the smallest ego crusher he

had, and he had disjointed every joint in my body; he had tortured me and forced me to reveal the secret of who I am. Who I had been?

Hadn't I been one of the mad people who practiced/played DuSable High School football on the gravel-covered lot adjacent to our school? Had I not survived many Chicago winters and the Bowen Hotel? *And* the Amo Hotel? Hapkido forced me to look at my backspacing a little harder. I detected a bit of puzzlement in the Master's eyes; it was obvious that he didn't know a lot about my kind of person.

"Where are you from?"

"Chicago."

"Ohh."

The influx of the other students prevented us from knowing each other better, but not before he had pulled out a photo of his wife-to-be (waiting-patiently-in-Korea for him-to-conquer-America).

"She will be my wife."

I stared at the photo, trying to bubble up the right comment to make about the Master's wife-to-be. Would he stab me with his forefinger if I said she looked like an Inglewood High School cheerleader? Or would he twist my ankle off if I suggested that she looked like a Korean version of Tina Turner?

"Nice?"

"Uhh, yes, nice."

The nightly ordeals suddenly seemed less cruel. Or was it my imagination? The student influx was a bit trippy. An LAPD hardnose (a pre-Rodney King brutality advocate) who had studied under Master Lee in Korea, in the army. A six-foot-tall, beer-bellied white guy who often foamed at the corners of his mouth, freaked out by the pain threshold he could legitimately take you over. No one wanted to be paired off with the "LAPD" (that's what we nicknamed

20

him) for holds, throws, or take downs. The man was totally crazed. Totally.

A charming collection of Korean youngsters aged ten to twelve (their parents insisted that they attend, to destabilize nascent American values), including Paulo and Henrique, a couple of Korean boys from Rio de Janeiro, Brazil. They thought the whole Korean-Korean/Korean-American number was being taken much too seriously. It was obvious to everyone that the Brazilian temperament had altered their Korean development.

"Why do we have to do this?"

"Mah!"

"What's that mean?"

Real cultural misfits (sometimes they spoke to each other in Portuguese); at eleven and twelve, they spoke better Portuguese than Korean and had quick eyes for the steatopygous Latinas who passed the dojang's window.

"Hey! I'm tired of this stuff! People choking me 'n trying to throw me across the room!"

The Brazilians had the fattest absentee record in the history of the dojang. Never a full week with the brothers on the scene.

Liberian brother came into it (feel tempted to spell it "It," but that might be misunderstood) for a few hot minutes and might've been good, but he couldn't stand the crotch stretches we had to do. I can still hear the virgin screams he made when his legs were being pushed east and west.

A young white man named Jeffrey (an accountant, for God's sake!) gave me a chance to give off my first serious case of hostility. Lord only knows what had been building up in me for a year.

In retrospect, I think it was an innate Black-man/Whiteman hostile number, and it was over in four punches; he punched me once and I punched him three times.

Master Lee cooled us out with a gentle little speech.

"No problem, OK?"

I was bitterly disappointed (for a half hour or so) at not being allowed to fight Jeffrey to the bone. After a year under the wings of the "Terrorist" (one of the Brazilians had given the Master his definitive nickname), I wanted to take my mean streak out on somebody. The heat was chilled.

Master Lee's dojang and rep quietly bloomed. We were a student body of twenty (twenty-two when the Brazilians showed up), and sometimes old Korean men, aficionados of hapkido, would stroll into the dojang to observe the action.

They made oblique observations, to be sure, but it was obvious that they were puzzled by the effect of Hapkido on African-American, "hispanic," "western" minds. They stood with their hands clasped behind their backs, slightly bent, alert.

I felt powerful. I knew how to throw a two-hundred-pound man over my back (I loved throwing the LAPD crazy man on his ass); I could kick a split in a piece of wood; I could twist a strong man's arm into a pretzel; and I was a red belt in an art form I'd never heard of 'til the year before.

I looked around in vain for Master Lee, the "Terrorist," who had made it all happen, but he was gone. It happened that suddenly; no great goodbye speeches, no final words, zip. One day he was there—"Mah!"—torturing us with twists of the wrists, arms, heads, legs, mind, when he wasn't kicking holes in our bellies, and the next day he was gone. Whiff!

He had "sold" us to Master Won Chang Lee; the dojang had changed hands.

Somebody said he went to work for the FBI: "You know—training agents."

22

I stayed home and sipped Beaujolais Villages (Trader Joe's had just imported a hundred thousand bottles) for a week, brooding for my Master. I had no idea how deep our bonding had been until he split the scene. This was the man who had taken us to perform for a petered-out Anglo-mall bunch in Canoga Park, who had given me casual instructions to leap into the air (jumping sidekick) and split a board held by four of my fellow students.

"You didn't kee-i," Jeffrey complained sourly. "You should have kee-i-ed."

Fuck you, Jeffrey. I couldn't believe it. Me? Breaking a board with my foot?! That was the stuff I came across in *Black Belt* magazine, whenever I read it. I recalled the tortured hours I had spent with him, my arms shackled by boa constrictor holds, being flung halfway across the dojang.

The week finally bungeed to an end; I was still a red belt in hapkido (no one can de-belt you), and I had to return to the scene.

Master Won Chang Lee didn't bear the slightest resemblance to his predecessor. He was wiry-lean, about five-foot-eight, his hair plastered into a permanent Valentino gloss, a couple of gold teeth in his upper fronts, cool.

He stressed the contemplative side of his art form: "Everybody kneel, close eyes, think Nothing."

Some of us took to Master Lee right off. I took to him because he was such a charming man. He charmed us into working just as hard with him as we had worked for the other Master Lee.

Aside: He also charmed the small, sex-foxy Korean lady who owned the mom 'n pop store next door. I checked her out making tight little runs from her place to his place, after both establishments had closed down for the night. It was all purely circumstantial, but that was enough to convince me and a couple other adult male spies that the lay-die's developing bay window was a sexual spinoff. "Wowww! I thought we were moral people!"

I suspect a whole bunch of secretly stored stereotypes were flushed down the drain during my first year with Masters Lee and Lee.

Number one: there was nothing inscrutable happening; if you wanted to find out what was happening behind the "mask," all you had to do was peek around the side.

"Mah!"

The Koreans struck me as being tenacious (a trait most Africans in America are definitely familiar with), somewhat reserved (with each other and others), positive thinkers, fully committed to getting as many goodies as they could get, one way or another.

It was also quite obvious that they preferred light skins to dark skins and they weren't/aren't particularly interested in African-American American history or circumstances....

In 1971 only the Census Bureau, or maybe Immigration, knew how many Koreans were living in Los Angeles. It definitely would have been impossible to say how many immigrant Korean merchants were scurrying to grab hold of liquor stores in South Central Los Angeles.

Yeah, it was pretty much like that. Evidently someone had tipped the Korean entrepreneurs off to the fact that the Africans in Watts loved booze, fake hair, cardboard shoes, and God only knows what else....

The info about what brand of cheap wino-liquor to sell was clearly revealed, and the proper shade of lipsticks and what kind of clothes we wanted to buy, but no one seems to have informed the entrepreneurs of the nature of the people they wanted to earn their profits from or how they should attempt to deal with them.

I had vague suspicions that a volatile mix was brewing.

24

Chapter 3

Master Won Chang Lee, like his predecessor, was a beautiful teacher—patient, involved, clear—but he was a poor businessman. Jeffrey, the accountant, cued me in.

"Master Lee is about to go under."

"How do you know?"

"He had me do his books. The poor guy'll be lucky if he winds up with a net loss of ten dollars this month. The other Master Lee dropped the business in his lap just before he was about to belly up."

Another stereotypical bit bit the dust: All Asian entrepreneurs (and specifically Koreans) were supposed to be A-1 businessmen. The Masters Lee hadn't bought into the game with the right cards, obviously.

We watched the fumbling and bumbling, listened to the incomprehensible gutteralings.

"Hey Paulo, what was the Master and that gangster lookin' guy talkin' about?"

"Master wanted to borrow some bread to keep the dojang going, but the juice man's rates were too high."

We practiced in semi-darkness a few times before the practice schedule was pushed up a few hours to take advantage of the daylight hours. Something decidedly uncool was happening between the Master and the light company.

"Everybody kneel, close eyes, think Nothing."

What with it all, the man was a rock. If Master Jun Bai Lee's job had been to inform us of the passion of hapkido, Master Won Chang Lee's job was obviously to show us the pride of the art.

Fantastic, the way it was done. The Master never lined us up and said, "This is it y'all; I'm not makin' enough dough to take care of my family, run this martial arts business, and do dojang," on a piece of paper and gave it to us. Once again, a Master had left me. The Korean experience was preparing me for lots of emotional changes.

Speaking of changes...

Some of my friends thought I was going into some kind of "bamboo fever" when I started asking for some advice about what I should do about this Okinawan woman I'd met in San Francisco.

"Wait a sec, pal. Run this by me one mo' time. You're tryin' to tell me that you're gonna leave this tried 'n true woman, whose expertise has helped you make money, that you've traveled halfway 'round the world with—and God only knows what else!—to hook up with some lil' ol' wrinkle-skirted bohemian oriental broad you've met in Frisco?"

"I think I'm in love with the woman, Chico."

"How in the fuck you gon' be in love with someone you just met last week?"

"I think it was love at first sight."

"Does she love you?"

"I'm pretty certain she doesn't. But, to be honest about

26

it, I don't really think she knows what love is anyway."

"Sounds like you got a strong case of bamboo fever to me. You need to get plenty of bed rest, lots of hot chicken soup, and breathe deep to clear your head up."

Of course, there were other opinions.

"You outta your fuckin' mind, man!"

None of it mattered to me. I had accidentally met the woman I wanted to be with and that was that. I was gon' be with her and that was that. I was gon' be with *that* woman.

Immediately after I reached that decision all kinds of complications set in, naturally. The first complication concerned the problem of dealing with the woman I have been living with for six years.

"Marlene, I have to leave you; I have to go off and be with this other woman."

"Beg your pardon?"

"I'm sorry, baby, I really am, but it seems that that's what I have to do."

It seemed bizarre, this urge, but logical to me. I had reached a peak with Marlene. We had worn Mexico out, tripped through northern Europe, and explored Compton together. It was time for another outline, another book, another atmosphere.

I'm tempted to say, being aware of how aware she was, that she understood where I was coming from. How do you bring yourself to say: "Uhhh, look, baby, it ain't about falling out of love with you or anything like that; it's just that I've found a new novel to write and if I don't write it, it'll get away from me."

How was I doing? I was doing quite well. I was deep in the middle of a writer's feast. I was living with the right woman (all African-American men writers should take careful note). I was on my third or fourth commissioned screen-

27

play (Gilbert Moses had been imported to direct). We were renting a gorgeous two-bedroom house, complete with fireplace and vineyarded back yard. I had three high profile African-American female lovers and I think I was "happy."

"Hey man!" Eric Priestley here. "Are you happy?" You have to answer questions from ex-Watts Writers Workshop compadres....

"Yeah, I think so."

What else could I say? I had the time (denied most beings who punch clocks or get snuffed out for "scientific" reasons) to take the time to feel out what was happenin' in my motherfuckin' life.

Well, OK, I'm going to hapkido; I must do that because it would be blasphemous not to. But hapkido has cut me loose and steered me into tae kwon do (whatever the fuck that is). Concurrently, I'm trying to reconcile these two women I want to have in my life. Yes, I did want to have my cake and eat it too.

Lady had run away to Hawaii...." I'm scared of you, of all of it."

Marlene, a European fatalist, had drawn the lines. She still loved me but was not into accepting bullshit. Awright, where is the bitch? I'll salute her with flowers in a civilized manner (dinner at Figaro's), offer her delicate tumble-weedlings, and get on.

Meanwhile, there is Alan Fishe ("Fishe, with an e, Alan, why?" "'Cause I don't want my children to be saddled with Fish.") and the movies.

The movies were fun. Alan Fishe helped make them fun. This was the mad producer that all up and coming writers should get to know, not the other kind. A mad producer. The right kind.

"Alan, are you loaded?"

"Why do you ask?"

28

"Because you're straddling the white line!"

Yeah, he made the Hollywood scene funny. I was "hot"; Hollywood was sliding into Blaxploitation time, and they wanted fuel for their machinery.

Alan, loaded on marijuana, psilocybin, peyote, cocaine, LSD, percodan, benzedrine, dexedrine, and chutzpah, was a designated talent finder.

He found me.

"Look, I'm working for Movienation Industries, we want you to write a couple screenplays for us."

The transition from Marlene to Lady had to be put on hold for a minute. I was madly in love but I wasn't stupid. I knew that I needed Marlene's expertise more than I needed Lady's hugs and moans.

"Sure. I'd like to write a couple screenplays for you guys."

A screenplay? What the fuck do they look like? It didn't really matter. The one thing I knew is that I was not going to write one of those disgraceful high-tech Stepin Fetchit things.

And I was not going to write a Sidney Poitier-Mammy Jemima movie (*Guess Who's Coming to Dinner*, *Patch of Blue*, *Lilies of the Field*, *The Defiant Ones*), any of the things he did while being holier than the white folks). I was going to write some shit they hadn't been exposed to, and Alan Fishe was going to help me get over.

I got immediately busy on *Eli's Games*, the story of an African-American con man who proves that his street level games could be elevated, immediately, to upper echelon board-room cheating simply by altering the jargon.

Alan was a powerful ally. We'd go to meetings in the Black Tower, and he'd be so fucked up and talking so much crazy shit it was scary. We'd come away with concessions that the assholes who rule the movies (still the same bunch

29

since then, younger) had never made before.

"Oh, you want Be Bop Bopha the fifth to direct? Never heard of him."

"Salad frosted in the oven hot diggedy on my toast all praise to the can opener, you shit."

"So, he's done all of those things, huh? Well, what the hell. Alan, if you think he can do it, we'll take the chance."

"Be Bop mop mop hip hop avan'garde."

There was more to it than that, of course. Alan Fishe was one of them and that helped. He was a pre-baby mogul, and I think that they felt good about humoring him. What the fuck, it was a good investment. If he managed to pull off a hot one with a budget of less than a mil, they'd make money. If his shit with the underclass wound up stinkin', they could write it off with the kids' summer camp experiences.

Nothing mattered to me; I was crazed by the drippin' drama. We had offices for the up 'n coming production at Universal; I was calling my sugar cane baby in Hawaii ("When you comin' back to the mainland, baby?"), making a transition from hapkido to tae kwon do, and stuffing as much coke up my nostrils as I possibly could.

It was a strange time. So strange.

So strange I had to put hapkido/tae kwon do on the back burner for a sec, to take a location trip to Chicago with Alan Fishe.

It had reached that point: Universal was going to do it where it happened. We tripped off to Chicago—Alan, me, and the big ol' Sebastian Cabot looking guy who was going to oversee our activities on Universal's behalf.

They were giving it to us, the whole avocado (of course they did this for themselves all the time): the suites in the Drake Hotel (where I had once worked as a delivery boy in the hotel's drugstore), the pocket money to be used as we could use it.

Alan Fishe wasn't a really bad guy to run around the Southside with. I mean, the people in the Palm Gardens thought he was kinda "cute."

That's what I heard one of the sisters say, staring at his tennis shoes (it was January in Chicago)—"He's kinda cute, ain't he?"

Interesting trip. Imagine, going back to where you had starved, fought, and frozen halfway to death, with a pocket full of money, some nice clothes on your back, and a purpose in mind.

"Mah!"

"Everybody kneel, close eyes, think Nothing."

The hapkido lessons focused my attention on shit that I hadn't ever paid any attention to before.

I became aware of the stranglehold Hollywood had on the African-American image. It didn't really matter if I wrote the greatest fuckin' screenplay in the history of screenplays, it was still going to be considered merely a "black screenplay."

Alan wasn't a racist dog or anything; he was just simply a cog in the machinery. He was going to get what he had to get from me. They could always change whatever I wrote. It was in the contract; my agent had made sure of that. I stood in the window of my suite, staring down at Oak Street Beach, cursing all the hours I had spent delivering codeine based cough syrup to all of the old fucked up, peely skinned white women, the summer evenings I was forced to hurry and deliver ice cream before it melted.

I practiced my hapkido exercises; they gave me something solid to hold on to. I felt the chi a few times, just breathing the right way.

And suddenly the trip home was over. We had gone to the pool room on 47th and Calumet; we had strolled through

31

43rd Street (from Cottage to King Drive before the usual suspects had been rounded up), stopped to stare into the keloided faces of brothers and sisters I had suffered with. It was wild. We'd spend the day thumbing through the black spaces on the near Southside and finish up the evenings with snifters of thirty-year-old cognac (Arc d' Triomphe) and six-day-old cocaine.

The trip was over. It was time to return to the coast, time to get serious, get into the fifth draft of *Eli's Games*, work black magic on the Universal Studios parking lot.

I felt terrible. I was in excellent physical shape (cocaine is a great aid in bodybuilding), but my head was fucked up. I'd go stand in front of the hapkido dojang after hours, knowing that classes were over. Hell, the place was closed; we had been re-routed to the tae kwon do dojang (whatever the hell that was), but I found it hard to give up my luxurious habits.

We had a man (could've been a vegetable man, selling stuff from the back of his truck) who came through the offices at Universal Studios selling tablespoons of cocaine for fifty dollars.

"Cocaine! Cocaine! Cocaine for sale! Pharmaceutical pure! Ninety-eight percent! Cocaine for sale!"

Fifty dollars for a heaping tablespoon of shit. Women in the typing pool were running up four-hundred-dollar tabs; executives barely took note of their habits until they had reached the five-thousand-dollar level.

I had put my transfer from hapkido to tae kwon do on hold for a minute so that I could coke as much as I wanted to. I felt guilty, to be sure, but I knew I was going to feel a hell or a lot guiltier if I tried to toot and go to the dojang at the same time.

That was one of the hard things I had learned about the dojang: it was a mean-assed motherfucker when it came to

32

doing what had to be done in there. It didn't pay to go in with your tongue hanging out (from excessive sexing, high-level boozing, or midnight hours) because the dojang regime would get up on you.

There were no exceptions or excuses; you came with the understanding that you were there to give it up or you didn't come.

I used the "transitional minute" (actually six to eight months) from hapkido to tae kwon do to do coke. Many of us called it "girl" or "white girl" then. It helped to be in a movie studio setting to do cocaine. The place was unreal, which made everything happening on the premises seem unreal. It didn't seem real that someone would be giving me thousands of dollars to do what I was going to do any-way. It should've been many *more* thousands than I received, but I didn't know that then.

My egomania was fed ground-shaking jolts of voltage by the coke. I even got to the point of telling the people paying me to go fuck themselves. They didn't know what to make of it. It was a hundred times worse with mere mor-tals. I was seducing Jehovah's Witness women—"Don't gimme that holy holy shit! I want to stick my dick in your ear."

"In my ear?! Oh my God! I never heard of anything like that!"

"Well, you've heard of it now. Commere 'n strip."

I was, however, extremely circumspect, and I can think of only three people who could've blown the whistle on me.

I didn't hang out with the movie crowd, didn't "do lunch" at the latest place or swing with the swingers. It was a sort of perverted undercover job with me.

"Look, I'm a man with odd desires; can you help me?"

I raided church socials, societies for the preservation of

33

Man, stuff like that.

"My, my, what a bold man you are."

"What's that got to do with you fuckin' me for the next hour?"

The "girl" took me into women and power writing. It would be difficult for me to recall what I was writing at the time (the screenplay, I conceded, was not mine; it was a "collaborative" effort), but I can clearly recall each of the thirty-six women I danced around. It wasn't always sexual. There were times when I simply felt the need to talk with a woman about being a man. I don't know why.

I wasn't freebasing (crack was up the road) and my habit was manageable at a grand a month, but I felt weird all the time. I was the ghetto bred brother who had frowned at the silly-ass dope fiends shooting low-grade heroin, formed a moral attitude about the winos on my block—idiots! And there I was with my cute little spoon and vial. The Universal Studios cocaine salesman had the best blow in town, and I ran up to the studio for my supply every day.

I wonder if he was subsidized by the studio. No telling; I found out about a bunch of strange scenes on the back lot. From time to time, unable to make my run, I'd make a buy from a local. I didn't find the same quality (from Beluga to shadfish roe) at the street level, which prevented me from having problems with "undesirable" characters. The Universal man was my man.

Strangely, I continued doing the breathing exercises and the muscle warping stuff that I had learned in hapkido. I must have been the best conditioned cokehead in Hollywood. Coke mania and coke macho ran me like a slave cylinder. I'd travel for an hour to make a party, stay ten minutes, and push gentle people out of my way to get back to my lines of nose candy.

I played Mussolini under the influence, a whole lot of

34

times: Brother invites me to speak to his creative writing class (twenty-five students, ten guests). "Why me?" "'Cause you're a successful screenwriter, a role model."

Me? A role model. Wowwwww....

I must've spent three days preparing my talk and tripled up on my coke intake (and supply). I wanted to be ready to say whatever my tongue had in mind; the "girl" told me I could do it.

"OK, you all know who I am but I don't know who you are and I don't want to know; you know why, simple, because there's about a thousand chances to one that ninety-nine percent of you so-called writers are just practicing a different form of masturbation anyway.

"I can look around this room and see the standard types: Miss Cutsy Pootsy over there, Mr. Black Ass Hemingway in the front, a couple crybabies who don't do anything but whine whine in print, the couple who think that writing is a substitute for the group therapy shit that they've been addicted to for so long, the so-called "Black Militant" who's been screaming page after page of 1960s rhetoric since 1961."

I can still remember the spectrum of expressions that settled on my face.

"What do you want me to say? Bless your precious little hearts because you've come in out of the cold, copped yourself a typewriter, and now you're ready to roll. I say fuck you! That's what I say. If any one of you motherfuckers comes within a mile of my shit I'm gonna try to burn a hole in your ass. Is that clear?"

A few people nodded. That wasn't satisfactory to me. I wanted complete acceptance.

"I said, "'Is that clear?'"

A few more people nodded, a number of them growled like Dobermans, a couple young brothers in dashikis stood

35

up and started applauding. I don't know why and didn't give a fuck; the coke had double-clutched and kicked me into fourth.

"You jive-ass poot-butt, it pains me in the red part to stand up here trying to talk, to waste my time on a bunch of cornfed chumps who ain't got it. I can look at you and tell you ain't got it. Well, OK, I'll be generous. How many people in this class? Forty, forty-five? I'd say there might be two of you in here who can stay the course.

"If the rest of you intellectual clowns had any sense of self-worth and respect for the craft of writing, you'd get off the pot right now, try to get a job teaching school or something, and get out of the way."

It went on like that, they told me, for about forty-five minutes before I stopped. I remember stopping, and the beginning, but the middle is a white darkness in my mind. It was easy to stop: my mouth suddenly shut and I didn't have anything else to say.

My friend Dean, the creative writing instructor, just shook his head back and forth in a puzzled way, saying, "Damn! I don't know whether to hug you or kick your ass."

Two members of the class, a female weightlifter (ever see a woman with muscles between her thumbs and forefingers?) and her Neanderthal looking boyfriend cornered me in the parking lot afterwards. It wasn't much of a contest. They wanted to fight and I wanted to get back to this Peruvian shit I had stashed at the house.

I pushed my fingers in the weightlifter's eyes and kicked the Neanderthal in the nuts. Some people thought it was wrong to do what I did. In any event, I was hot on the lecture circuit for a minute; guess they wanted to see if I'd go off and play monster-man again. I didn't consciously make an effort to do the monster thing; it was just a sort of Jekyll-and-Hyde number that sprang out whenever I found myself

36

talking to more than five people under the influence of "blow."

Number one: despite the nice lecture fee, I was terrified of speaking/lecturing. Number two: I was semi-crazed from snorting this shit up my nose. There was no way I can figure out why the cops in Watts (103rd and Avalon) didn't shoot me the night I jumped out of my car rantin' 'n ravin' about the racism and police brutality. Or at least beat me senseless, as was usually done back then.

Chapter 4

And some kind of luck had to be with me the night I faced off a trio of good ol' boys in San Bernardino dressed in Pendleton shirts and German helmets, with swastikas tattooed on their cheeks.

"Hey, the motherfucker was trying to run me down! It ain't my fault if he spilled off his bike."

"Joe Tom, you OK?"

It was about 4:00 AM and I was making my way back to L.A. from a coke-crazed weekend orgy with an African woman who lived in an area called "Whites Only."

"Why in the hell would you buy a house in Whites Only?"

"Nobody told me about it. I haven't had any problems so far."

"You've only been here four days."

"Boy, where you from?"

"Who in the fuck you callin' a boy, motherfucker?!"

"Joe Tom, you OK?"

"Yeah, I'll live. Looks like my dick got rubbed off on the ground though."

Joe Tom was obviously their favorite comedian or something because all of the attention was taken up with them laughing at him.

"Joe Tom, what the fuck made you try to ride your bike up that nigger's back like that?"

"Must've been this strong white blood runnin' through my veins."

"Hahh hahh hahh hahhah...."

And suddenly, ethereally, they were gone, blasted off on Harleys. I felt my legs rubberizing as I got back in my car to horn up a speedball. I had to get ready, they might come back. Irrationality ruled for ten minutes while I dug under the front seat for my stuff and tooted from the spoon. What the hell am I waiting for? What if they do come back? What will I do then?

I hurriedly put my stuff away and shot away from the roadside. I was doing about 110 when I shot past them ten miles up the road. Paranoia closed in on me. They're after me! They're gonna lynch me! They're gonna lynch me!

I shot into downtown L.A. like a rocket, wheeling and dipping through the downtown streets to throw them off my tracks. By the time the sun came up I must've driven for miles around the downtown skyscrapers, fleeing a trio of nonexistent bikers.

Pause on a side street for a little bump and a slow, victorious ride home.

Marlene didn't know what the fuck to do with me. I knew she had her own agenda worked out and it wouldn't be long before she finished typing the script and we'd have a friendly parting party and I'd hook up with the Okinawan woman, but meanwhile...

40

"Look, Alan, can't you see how fucked up this is gonna be if you let that asshole change this scene?"

"Which scene is that?"

"The Bergmanesque thing I have on page 50, scene 50, where Eli, the quintessential street hustler is dreaming—the 'dream scene' I'm calling it—that he's sitting behind a beautiful walnut desk, dressed in his beautiful clothes, doing beautiful business right there in the heart of the Westside, on the corner."

"I can see it, I like it; yeahhh, I like it."

"That's what you said when you first read it, so why are you going to let that motherfucker take it out and put some kind of dumb chase-shoot-'em-up in there?"

"'Cause he's the motherfucker with the bread and he wants a chase-shoot-'em-up right there."

"But it wouldn't make any sense right there."

"Look, man, can't you get it through your skull? It doesn't fuckin' have to make sense; it has to make money, that's all. And the Biggie wants a chase-shoot-'em-up 'cause he thinks it'll make money; get it?"

I got it. I doubled up on my coke toke. I would leave Universal Studios with three hundred dollars worth of coke (a lot then) and the urge to fuck my frustration away. That's all I wanted to do, toot and screw. Once again, I was being taken care of. That's the only explanation I can find for not acquiring one bad germ during the whole period. The ladies were top of the line all the way, to be sure, but even top of the line pussy can conceal wicked viruses 'n shit, especially if you're going from one to another.

If I had developed a case of clap during that time I would've been forced to call twelve people to get to the bottom of the pile. Where was I going the night I got stopped? Who knows where I was going? I didn't know. But I knew I had to pause for a toot: I knew that; that was

41

a definite thing.

Gas station on the northeast corner of La Brea and Olympic. Perfect. I popped out of my car, asked for a "filler up," and popped into the men's room for a little fuel of my own. I laid a couple lines out on a postcard—"See San Francisco"—rolled up the crisp twenty, and bent down to follow the white dragon's tail: one side and then the other, just like doing sidekicks.

"Snorrrret! Snorrrret!"

I straightened up slowly, enjoying the familiar icing of the nasal passages, the cool freeze in the frontal lobes, the money-straw poised and ready for future action. My dead mother stared out of the mirror above the washbasin at me.

"What the fuck are you doing?"

I don't know how long she stared at me because I dropped my eyes, unable to answer her question.

What the fuck am I doing? What the fuck was I doing?

I slowly opened the door, slowly walked to my car, paid the attendant, drove slowly home, and flush-poured fifteen hundred dollars worth of high-grade Bolivian cocaine down the toilet. I was ready to go on to tae kwon do. Yeahhh, right, talk about cold turkey....

I didn't realize what I had done until the next day, and then I got real anxious. How was I going to know how to act without my "girl?"

I asked the question of my head several times a day for a couple weeks and got on about my business. I didn't look back then, and I haven't since then. Momma's face in the mirror took care of the possibility of looking back.

Onward to this stuff that Master Wan Chang Lee had steered me into. I was eight months late, but I was going.

Hapkido has elements of akido and jujitsu in it; one grapples frequently. Tae kwon do is the "hand and foot" way, punching and kicking. The punches are designed to put your

42

lights out, the kicks are powered by the will to destroy. I entered Master Kim's dojang knowing as little about tae kwon do as I had known about hapkido. In addition to all of this instant involvement with Asian martial arts, I was on the cusp of solidifying my relationship with the Okinawan woman.

There was no correlation between my involvement with her and the martial arts. Unlike a number of brothers who had become involved with Asian women because of their craze for Asian martial arts, I got into a thang with her in spite of the martial arts; she could've cared less.

She was back on the mainland, up in Frisco, and I was in "El-A," when I wasn't runnin' up 'n down 101 to see her. I was trying to do everything: break up peacefully with Marlene, write another commissioned screenplay, sew it up with Lady Hilo, figure out how not to get killed in Master Kim's dojang, and swim through the pure pussy river that California had at that time.

Shit was exciting, but chaotic.

Marlene and I split. Lady Hilo was persuaded to move down to L.A. to be with me. Our romance was as vicious as the love-hate yin-yang between two alley cats. Ironically, that's where we sewed it up, at the end of a dead end street (Mariposa-butterfly) off of Santa Monica Boulevard, in an apartment complex filled with cats.

But that's getting ahead of ourselves...

"Hey man, you wanna take a drive to Frisco with me? I'll buy the gas and you'll be able to replenish your pussy supply." It was just about that simple. My artist friend needed to pick up something in San Francisco. I needed a break.

"Yeah, when you wanna leave?"

"Tonight?"

"Cool."

He went for his stuff and I went for Lady Hilo.

43

"Uhhh, this is Lady Hilo; I'll be back in a couple hours."

That's about all it took for the "cat fight" to start. We drank Metaxa, smoked dope, ate Mexican food (La Barca's, on Lombard Street), and made divine love for two days.

"Uhhh, say, look, brother man, I know the pussy is exquisite 'n all that but I got a family down in L.A. and they're missing me. You know what I mean?"

"I know, I know; we'll leave this afternoon for sure."

The only solution we could see was for her to move to L.A., into the "cat house" on Mariposa, off Santa Monica Boulevard.

"Line up! Line up! Everybody line up! Quickly! Quickly!"

Master Kim's dojang was within walking distance of our apartment. I was expected to attend class three nights a week and sometimes on Saturday morning. Master Kim was the Godfather and Herman da Silva was his right hand man and primary instructor.

It was a great time for exploration. I was exploring a wire-meshed jungle of things: life without cocaine, life with a nineteen-year-old Hawaiian-Okinawan-Japanese-American hippie (I was thirty-six). We were exploring the possibilities of blowing dynamite smoke through our nostrils, what it would be like to kill each other with misguided passion. I think we both thought it odd that we didn't want to kill each other with axes and knives.

The basic difference with us, as opposed to my relationship with Marlene (and her look-alike white guys) is that I felt no urge to come home from a strenuous evening at the dojang and take out my hostility on Sister Hilo. It was so subtle, the shit they were doing to me, that she seemed to have nothing to do with what we were doing in the dojang. I would never be able to honestly say that that was the way I felt after I left a meeting with chez whitey.

44

I'm leaving a "business meeting" ("I'm going to rod your ass out with a Eurocentric rotor rooter and ask you to like it") with chez whitey (SEE LIVING COLOR), and I feel that I'm choking with bad vibes, forcing me to spew up shit that I didn't even know I had in me. (The brothers who deal with chez white-motherfuckers who come home to make love to one of chez whitey's sisters have to be considered sexual geniuses.)

The difference, I think, between meeting with chez whitey and having my ass kicked in the Asian arts is that I was forced to look at my mistakes, not reflect other mistakes. Maybe Koreans planned it that way; they *are* a clever group of people.

The transition was effective. Marlene had met Lady Hilo at Figaro's on Melrose Avenue, with a delightfully arranged bunch of flowers, turning my angry, weird, black ass over to her.

If the truth really has ring to it, it didn't seem right that they'd sit there, drinking wine and talking about all the shit they knew about me. It wasn't flattering. Secretly, like any other freaky writer, I thought I'd seen a li'l hostility, maybe a deep frown or two.

I had to separate them as soon as possible; they were immediately on the verge of becoming friends. Damn!

Well anyway, fuck it! I'm still a writer with stuff to say; I've changed women but I still have work to do, and I still have to pay my dues in the tae kwon do dojang. Why? I don't have the slightest idea. I'm there because the hapkido dojang closed and the Master sent me over to this place. Isn't it interesting how interesting some interesting shit can be?

Like I said earlier, I didn't know any more about tae kwon do than I did about hapkido, and that was going to make a difference in tae kwon do. It took me a few weeks

45

to come to grips with that understanding, but tae kwon do is a very understanding art.

"Line up! Everybody line up!"

Hapkido had transferred me; Marlene had passed me on; and tae kwon do was nurturing me after a coke binge that could've really fucked up my whole life. I felt grateful. The dojang was spacious, well lit; the subterranean stuff was missing, and the classes were tough but manageable.

How many times did I go to class singing, my gym bag full of freshly thought feelings? It was no bad reflection of Master Jung Bai Lee or Master Won Chang Lee that I felt I was in a better place. It had space! You could breathe! And the teaching was not oppressive.

Master Kim was the Godfather, but he gave the day-to-day instruction over to Herman da Silva, black belt extraordinaire. Master Kim was the breath that filled Herman da Silva's lungs.

How old was he? Twenty, twenty-two years old. And his whole life had been spent learning tae kwon do under/from Master Kim. He couldn't get enough of tae kwon do. As it was told to me, he had followed Master Kim to America, to continue his apprenticeship and to teach under his direction. It was a weird setup to a lot of our westernized minds. Why would a person who was as eminently qualified to teach as he was continue to be Master Kim's student?

A few advanced types tried to explain it to us but it never fully registered. Herman da Silva: the name became interwoven in my head with devotion to one's chosen art.

"Line up! Everybody line up quickly! Quickly!

He was "movie star" handsome, and the ladies (Asian and otherwise) who were bold enough to take the class spent a lot of time mooning and swooning over him. They also spent a lot of time panting and groaning because he didn't give a shit how much they mooned and swooned, they still

46

had to do the sit-ups and sidekicks too. I had reached the red-belt level in Hapkido, which would've meant that I was a candidate for black belt in tae kwon do. I was *not* a candidate for a black belt in tae kwon do. I was simply wearing the belt rank from a related art.

Nobody said shit to me. Nobody said, "Hey buddy, when you change from one style to another, you should start at white belt again."

Da Silva didn't say anything; he just kicked the shit out of my ass for weeks. We sparred frequently in Master Kim's dojang, and for weeks I tried to figure out how to grab hold of somebody so that I could throw them down and strangle them.

It wasn't happening, especially with Herman da Silva. I could defend myself from the other students but not from Herman.

On one memorable evening I established a record for being kicked in the stomach, bowled backwards with a finely honed front snapkick, courtesy of Master da Silva. Fifteen times, twenty times he punched me in the stomach/chest with his foot. And I was determined to get past the punishment zone to get one punch in, just one. It didn't happen that night. It took me weeks to figure out that I was doing something wrong. When you have problems in tae kwon do, you go talk with your instructor.

"Herman, what am I doing wrong?"

"You're trying to fight hapkido style, to grab and throw. This is tae kwon do; we kick and punch."

"Oh."

I immediately retired the red belt from hapkido and got about the business of learning tae kwon do from scratch. I also began to pay more attention to the Koreans who were teaching me this art. In the hapkido dojang I hadn't noticed certain things, or rather I should say I had been oblivious

47

to a lot of stuff. I hadn't noticed the racism, for example. It was because of my "ancient age," obviously, that Master Kim decided to focus on me as a source of American information. I could tell I was in for some diplomatic problems after the first session.

"Ahh, Mr. Chester, come in office after class."

"You wanted to see me, Master Kim?"

"Yes, sit. You tell me why black people drink so much?"

I wasn't stunned by the abruptness of the question; I had discovered that tae kwon do was like that—right to the chin. I was tripped out by the nature of the question.

"Why are there so many Korean liquor store owners?"

We stared at each other for a moment, his question still bonging in my head, my answer still clanging around his head. I wasn't completely satisfied by my answer and decided that I'd be better prepared for future questions, when and if they came. It didn't take long. The next practice session...

"Mr. Chester, come in office after class."

Damn! Now what? When you finish getting your ass cracked on somebody's heel for an hour and a half, you want to peel off, take a shower, down a cold one, do the do.

"You wanted to see me, Master Kim?"

"Yes, sit. You tell me your idea of this question."

Master Kim was a charming man with eyes like an elf and a mind that was cobra venom quick. He made up his English as he went along.

"You are ready for question?"

"Yessir."

"Black man see white man with black woman, he is angry. Why?"

"How do Korean men feel when they see Korean women with Japanese men?"

I made him smile sometimes. I think he began to appre-

48

ciate the shorthand I was using. It had occurred to me, early on, that it would be crazy to try to take him through African-American history, in order to explain anything. He didn't want to hear it.

"Mr. Chester, George Washington, father...of country. You like?"

"No sir, George Washington was a slaveowner; I've never liked slaveowners."

I began to ask some questions of my own (not of Master Kim but of others). The Brazilians who had transferred from the hapkido dojang with me were a couple fountains of knowledge.

"Hey Paulo, Henrique, tell me something. What was Master Kim saying to Jimmy Suh?"

"He said to him, you are doing a sidekick like an American dog lifting his leg on a fire hydrant."

"An American dog?"

"That's what the man said."

Some of the stuff was so out there it was hard to know whether to be pissed about it or not. The chauvinism was more easily and clearly understood.

Master Kim, in an after-practice speech, one of hundreds he made over the years... "If woman in home is not doing right, man must give her a little medicine!"

The chopping motion he made with his right hand made it quite clear what "medicine" was. All of the Americans in the dojang groaned with distress at such sexism.

Master Kim looked bewildered.

"Mr. Chester, office after class."

"Yessir?"

"Sit, sit.... I have question."

"Yes, I know."

"You tell me what you are thinking of this?"

"Yessir."

"Black people in United States are not working all together. Why?"

"Are all of the Koreans in the United States working together?"

I was able to recommend a bunch of books to him, and I suspect that he may have read a few because his questions became increasingly sophisticated over the years. It didn't really make a great impact on me for a while, this Korean right-wing prejudiced thinking, until I casually put a question to Henrique one evening. Herman da Silva, good-looking dude, bet he must have pussy in storage 'til he can get to it, no matter how much evidence of celibacy I see.

"Hey, Henrique, who is Herman's lady?"

"Herman ain't got no lady."

There was something about the way he said it. Was Herman gay?

"What's that mean, he ain't got no lady?"

Brother Paulo, standing nearby, toweling off; they were twelve and thirteen now, going on twenty and thirty, wise old heads.

"He ain't got no lady. You dense or somethin'? Look, the guy's father is Portuguese and his mother is Korean."

"Yeah, I know that, but what's that got to do with it?"

The two young men stared at me like I was the dumbest person they'd ever tried to explain something to.

"Paulo, you explain it to him."

"OK, look, the guy ain't Portuguese and he ain't Korean, OK?"

The light was coming on in my dimness.

"Remember the Korean college girl who was coming to class twice a day, every day last month—what was her name, Henrique?"

"The one with the big cabashahs? Her name was Suzy Hae."

50

"OK, this Suzy was hot for Herman, right?"

"Obviously; a blind man could see that."

"Where is she now?"

"She dropped out."

"Her parents pulled her out. The word had gotten back to them. Suzy had the hots for this half-breed tae kwon do guy named Herman. No good. Got it? No good."

I strolled west on Santa Monica, thinking hard on the absurdity of the racism. Herman was their best (some people argued that he would've kicked Bruce Lee's nuts out of socket); he was Mr. Tae Kwon Do. Why would they discriminate against him?

They discriminated against him because he was "mixed." Shit, everybody is mixed. The racism was absurd, but no more absurd than any other racism.

Chapter 5

Life in the cat house. Lady Hilo and I had found an apartment at the end of a dead end street, a two-story complex with huge ferns in the courtyard area, managed by a horny, middle-aged white woman who housed and fed fifty-some-odd cats and a young Pacific Islander (I think he was from Tonga). The place reeked with cat piss ammonia and weirdass tenants.

"I don't think we're going to be here very long."

"Why not? I like this place."

We went at it like that for months; if I suggested that it was night, she would say, "Well, it's going to be day pretty soon, so there!"

If I hadn't been into tae kwon do I'm sure I would've kicked her ass. It was an odd situation in many ways (hindsight analysis coming up), this romance between the Hawaiian-born-Okinawan-Japanese-American hippie and me.

I could clearly see that some of the shit that was happening between us was a result of the age difference. She was rebelling at twenty. And I was rebelling at thirty-seven. The problem we had was that we were rebelling against different stuff. I was in a defy-America mode, and she was in a defy-Chester mode.

Lady Hilo, a New Asian, found herself in tandem with a New African, and I think that was hard for her to deal with. I kinda felt that she wanted me to be more authoritarian, a bit more rigid.

Fuck that shit; that wasn't where I came from and I was not going to play into it.

Strangely, I don't think cultural distinctions played a tremendous role in our differences of opinion. It didn't take an effort for me to get ready for sashimi and tempura, nor for her to get ready for Black music and love. We struggled with each other, but it never reached the *Who's Afraid of Virginia Woolf* stage, and we started pulling in the same direction after a while.

I think the turning point came when I woke up one morning and discovered that I was paralyzed. Weird feeling about being paralyzed; you can't swivel your ass around the way you want to.

"Chester, what's wrong?"

"I don't know, feels like my back is frozen."

She hopped out of bed to make me some tea while I reviewed the night before, trying to identify the source of my back problem. Tae kwon do. I had taken the usual amount of punishment, maybe a little more than usual, but that happened from time to time. Tae kwon do was always a pain, somewhere. This was different. I was paralyzed. The thought played tricks on my mind. I was paralyzed. Shit, I really was paralyzed.

"Can you move?" Lady Hilo asked.

The question struck me in such a funny way I laughed and loosened up a bit. We both laughed. What the hell else was there to do? Can you move? Well, I had loosened up to laugh at an absurd question; maybe I could keep on laughing and get out of bed at the same time. The lady must've thought I had lost my mind as I let loose with this manic laughing streak and rolled over the side of the bed at the same time.

"Chester, you're on the floor."

A new burst of laughter helped me pull myself to a kneeling position. My back was frozen, but I could move my arms and legs and I had a loving, concerned woman asking me funny questions. What to do? Go to the dojang, ask for help. How to get there? Hop on the stolen ten-speed I had just purchased a few days before from one of our fellow dope fiend tenants. We pulled off a comic-heroic departure scene as she helped me climb onto the bike.

"Are you going to be able to make it?"

"If I don't, I'll give you a ring."

"Ohhh, Chester, be serious."

"I am serious, baby, I am serious."

From Mariposa and Santa Monica Boulevard to Vermont and Santa Monica Place usually took five minutes. I don't know how long my trip took that day. I didn't have the slightest idea how I was going to dismount, once I arrived at the dojang. The law of gravity solved my problem: I fell off the bike and didn't have to bow, as usual, when I entered the front door. I was already bent. Blessed Herman da Silva was on the scene. He took one look at me and began dialing a number.

"This is the address of Dr. Bong Pil Roh; can you make it?"

The doctor was at Normandie and Hollywood Boulevard. I laughed myself back onto the bike and pedaled away. By this time I had reached a fatalistic stage: Fuck it! If I'm gonna die, I may as well die in the saddle. I pulled into the middle of Vermont (heading north) and revved myself up to a fast five miles an hour. Cars swept around me to pull in front of me but no one blew their horns. I guess they figured I was just another crazy in the fast lane. My dismount technique was almost perfect by now; I rammed the bike into Dr. Pil Roh's front porch and fell off. He opened the door about five inches as I crawled up the steps. He opened the door another couple inches to allow me to squeeze in. Rationally, I remember thinking what was the rationale for making me squeeze through the door?

It was not my imagination that made me feel this warm glow on my body as I squeezed through the door. I glanced into the doctor's eyes. They were gleaming as they swept from my waist to my neck. Herman da Silva had explained to him what my problem was and he was obviously doing a prelim x-ray with his eyes. A small, extremely wiry man with the face of a wise monkey. I felt safe.

"Where?" he asked, and pulled out a torso drawing. He handed me a pencil and indicated that I should shade in the distressed area. He stared at the figure after I had shaded in the entire back. He stared at me for a few minutes and smiled.

"I fix."

It was my first experience with acupuncture and it was extremely rewarding. After the nineteenth needle was spun into my body I was well on my way to the deepest sleep I'd ever had in my life. Suddenly Master Won Chang Lee's words—"Everybody kneel, close eyes, think Nothing"— meant something. I wasn't kneeling; I was flat on my belly on a table, but my eyes were closed and I thought Nothing. I thought Nothing for two more visits and my back was completely unfrozen. I was converted to the powers of

56

acupuncture. I returned to the dojang the minute I could bend and touch my toes. Something snapped in me, like pushing through a barrier. I had been paralyzed by the art; I wanted to get more deeply into it. I felt the urge to be a tae kwon do man.

Some weeks I would go to the dojang in the afternoon and evenings.

"Uhh, Chester, are you going to the dojang again?"

"Yeah, baby, I think I need to work a little harder on my sidekicks."

A bit of Herman da Silva and a lot of Master Kim was rubbing off on me. If you wanted to be good in tae kwon do, you practiced a little; if you wanted to be superior, you practiced a lot. I ignored the beautiful young Korean woman who fell in love with me (her name, translated, was "Green Jade").

"Chester, I am feeling my heart for you."

"Stop whispering and do your sit-ups. How many?"

The Korean parents, I discovered, had emotional tentacles that were like radar. "Green Jade" was whisked away the following month. I felt strangely proud; I was a kind of Herman da Silva, a few belts down. The dojang was where I went to fight, and the more I understood about the etiquette of the fighting, the more I enjoyed it.

Tae kwon do converts your legs into arms, your feet into fists. And then you still have the upper "legs" as fists.

The etiquette: Herman da Silva starts with the lower ranking belts—white, yellow, blue—giving them a chance to bow to each other and fling their feet out into the air for a few minutes.

"Stop!"

They turn away from each other to straighten their belts and doboks, turn back around to bow to each other again and run back to the side of the dojang to resume their half

57

lotus seats. It was fairly easy for me to go from white to green belt. It began to get hard when it got to brown. Brown, red, black.

"Chester!" Herman da Silva calls with a flick of his finger. I'm a brown belt now and he is not kicking my ass all over the place anymore. He is still kicking my ass, but I find myself capable of sticking a right hand into his gut from time to time.

Master Kim seldom spars, and when he does it's with Herman (thank the Lords). The contests are mongoose and weasel. They do some things so fast that they've happened before you realize they've happened.

People, personalities whizzed through the dojang; I stayed for six years. During the course of that time frame I fought the Nazi bitch. She could've been a Hitlerian ideal: sea blue eyes, yellow blonde, fanatical. She had gotten a black belt from another dojang and came into "our" place. Diplomatically, Master Kim and Herman da Silva never sparred with her; they gave me the dirty work to do. I used to tear her ass up every chance I got. It was unavoidable. From the moment she gave me her hate-filled look until I had punched a hole in her side usually took only a moment; it had to be because I sensed that her fanaticism would've overwhelmed me if it took longer.

Ironically, a Jewish guy was the one who alerted me to the fact that she was a Nazi.

"Did you see the swastika on that bitch's chest?"

"No, where?"

"On her fucking chest, low down on the left side. I saw it when her jacket fell open last night."

"Are you sure it was a swastika?"

"Hey, you think a guy named Bernstein doesn't recognize a swastika when he sees one?"

Nazi, lots of crazies, physical types who loved to do

58

push-ups but had no idea what tae kwon do was about and didn't really care so long as they were made to sweat enough. A lot of confused people looking for their place, their mommies, their daddies. A collection of folks searching for a group therapy, a few dedicated tae kwon do students.

I began to understand the Master Kim-Herman da Silva conspiracy. They were not into offering immediate rewards for flashy conduct; one had to earn the belt. It took me almost four years to earn the red belt. Tae kwon do is a way of life and they made damned sure you understood that before you were promoted.

We moved from the cat house to an apartment on the corner of Clinton and Van Ness. I was moving toward the black belt (an indication that you are beginning to understand something about the art, nothing more, nothing "mystical"), but Hollywood had taken a nose job on me.

My agent couldn't get me the gigs that he had once tossed my way so casually.

"Sorry, Chester, nothing yet, but we got a couple pots on the back burner." I heard that a lot in 1978.

Lady Hilo was playing waitress in an Italian restaurant, bringing home lasagna and enough tips to keep us from starving, but it was not the best of times. The ceiling in the apartment had a lot to do with the oppression we began to feel. It was only about five feet, ten inches from the floor to the ceiling. We could stand on tippytoe and touch the top of the living room. If that ain't oppressive enough, we have a nappy-headed Black cowboy-hippie living upstairs who thinks he's Mick Jagger on the piano.

The idiot feels inspired to get up and bang on the piano at odd times, usually after midnight. We didn't honestly know how to handle it for a while. Our sense of First Amendment rights and ACLU-righteousness forced us to

59

discuss him a lot.

"Have you talked to him?"

"I talked to him this afternoon."

Maybe it wouldn't've been so aggravating if the idiot could play the piano somewhat. But he couldn't play very well and *insisted* on playing, loudly.

It came to a murderous halt one Sunday morning. He stunned me awake from a mean streaked hangover.

"Chester? Chester? What're you going to do?! Oh my God!"

"Be right back; I've had enough of this shit."

I can imagine what the picture of an angry demon with swollen red eyes, carrying a Cuban born machete looks like. The musical dunce reflected that mirror when he opened his back door. I put the point of the machete in his chest and jabbed hard.

"One more note and your motherfuckin' head is comin' off."

He found a garage down the street to bang away in immediately thereafter. Meanwhile, the survival tango was retired and a hip swiveling mambo was put on the turntable.

"Chester, looks like you've got a feature length movie script to write for United Pictures, Ltd."

A movie script to write. I took a deep breath and let it out slowly. A movie script meant big bucks; we were over the hump.

60

Chapter 6

"United Pictures, Ltd." was one of those mid-sized movie studios that pushed a bunch of now famous actors through, specialized in "small" pictures (nothing artsy fartsy) that made money and was run by a guy who ate his salad with his fingers and sliced his steak up into small pieces at the beginning of the lunch.

"Now look, Chester, I want you to do what you do best, OK?"

"What's that mean?"

"We want you to come up with an idea for a feature film and write it. Simple."

Simple as that. I got busy. I was enthusiastic but I wasn't naive enough to believe that they were going to run with the ball I threw to them. But what the hell, why not try? I flung a Hail Mary to the shortest end I'd ever seen, the producer they had assigned to me/my project, a neurotic little bastard named Teddy.

"Now hold on here a fuckin' minute, Chester! You've got a first-draft script here about some kids who start a rehab/settlement/arts center in an empty building in the south Bronx? You want Redd Foxx, the *real* Redd Foxx, to play the director of the thing? You've written in a bunch of names nobody can pronounce...."

"They're Puerto Ricans; they live in the Bronx."

"One of the fuckin' guys is named Israel, for God's sake."

"One of them is named Jesus too."

"And you've got quotes from Malcolm X and Mao Tse Tung and who is this fuckin' Faye-non? What're you, some kinda fuckin' anti-Semitic commie bastard? I oughta put my foot up your ass!"

"I invite you to try it, pal."

It went like that at every meeting. After the third one I realized that they didn't want the "Ghetto Jet Set," with all of the satirical implications that the name suggested. Teddy and the boys were frothing for the usual "urban action" bullshit. They wanted it bad enough to sic one of their full-busted Dobermans on me; her name was Lucille.

"Chester, Lucille here; look babe, you've got Teddy and the gang all upset about your latest refusal to do the right thing. I think this whole business could be resolved in a weekend. Now, here's what I have in mind. I have a friend who has an absolutely gorgeous place in Acapulco. Why don't we get our swim caps and swim suits and go on down there this weekend and work this thing out to everybody's satisfaction?"

"Fuck you, Lucille!"

"How's that?"

"You heard me, I said fuck you!"

"That's not the right attitude to make it with United Pictures, Ltd."

"I know. I'm supposed to become a bitch-ho just like you to make it with United Pictures, Ltd., right?"

"Teddy will be speaking with you shortly; goodbye."

I didn't give a damn anymore. I had turned in three and a half versions of my vision and they had all been shot on.

"Chester! Are you outta your fuckin' gourd?! You think we're gonna bite ourselves in the ass?!"

"Teddy, I thought you asked me to write you a screenplay, something from my own experience."

"Yeah, but what's with all this fuckin' European stream-of-consciousness shit?"

"That's not European; it's an Africentrically-oriented stream-of-consciousness."

"Who gives a shit!? I don't want it! You understand me?! I don't want it!! I oughta kick your ass for putting me through this kinda bullshit!"

"If you dare bring your little fat ass from around that desk, I'm gonna fuck you up!"

Teddy baby was always threatening to beat me up. I found out from the security guard who "escorted" me from his office that he *had* kicked a few people in the ass.

"He bloodied one dude's nose. You know how it is when that cocaine is drivin' you."

"Yeah, brother, I know all about it; I know all about it."

"See ya later, brother. Oh, incidentally, you know you can't come in here no mo' unless you get a clearance."

"I figured as much."

I was relieved. I wasn't going to be forced to have any more phoney revisions to do. I wasn't going to be forced to put my anger in cold storage, nor would I have to worry about money for a few months. I could concentrate on getting the kata (forms) right for my tae kwon do black belt examination. I hated the kata, but I knew they had to be up to snuff if I wanted to get my belt.

My agent was pissed with me.

"Chester, why did you have to bust the guy's balls like that? Jesus Christ! What did you do?"

"I didn't do anything."

"Well, so be it, as they say. You've got a final payment coming from that last revision. I'll get it to you as soon as we get it. Meanwhile, I'll be peeking into a couple corners for you. Take it easy."

Hollywood was over for me; I could tell from the dripping tone of the agent's voice. "Take it easy." He'd never said anything like that before.

It was over and I was glad. What the hell, I had a total of six-seven movie scripts lying around on the shelves of each major studio in town, and one script in one middle-sized studio. It wasn't a bad record for a brother who came out of a basement on Washbourne, with no connections.

I hated to lose the money; I truly hated that. But I hated the suck-ass requirements that the producers had designed for the Hollywood screenwriters even more.

How can someone who is creating a "baby" (screenplay) be given an "assignment?" I hated the racism even more.

"Chester, Joan and I have read your outline and it's really neat.... She thought you were a white guy..., hah hah hah...."

"OK, let's git down, baby. Chester, is that the way a dude in the 'hood would say it?"

The overt shit was bad enough; the covert shit was even worse, *is* even worse.

"Now then, how much do we want to cheat this guy out of?"

"Why not the whole thing?"

"You mean, not pay him anything?"

"That's exactly what I mean. What's he gonna do, sue us?"

64

The Hollywood of those years remains unchanged. The scenery has been shifted a bit, but the focus is still basically myopic, racist, mean-spirited, artistically neutered by a systematic castration of any truly creative nature. Can you imagine what Hollywood would've done to Bergman? Fellini? Rossellini? What it did to Micheaux? Robeson? Ivan Dixon? Thousands?

Hollywood was/is Amerikkka (that's three ks) and Amerikkka is Hollywood, and I wanted to take a break, dammit! I needed a break, but first the black belt examination in tae kwon do.

Why should it seem different from all the other belt exams? The brown belt exam was tough. The red belt exam was tough, and, of course, the black belt exam is going to be just as tough. It couldn't be any tougher than the other examinations, but somehow it is. The flavor of the peer group makes it tougher. You are going to have a first degree taste of the spirit that haloes Bruce Lee's grave, and Master Jun Bai Lee's head, the Master Won Chan Lee's head, and Master Kim's head, and Herman da Silva.

There were six or seven of us going for the belt, and we had enough electricity crackling through us to light up the dojang. Everything had to be done exactly exactly. The bow, not too much or too little, each kick perfectly executed, the kata done with awareness (no robotic stuff for Master Kim and Herman), strength, and precision. The sparring was a high point of the exam. First, with one opponent, then two, then three. And a few other bits were added—questions from Master Kim.

"Is wrong or right to use tae kwon do on drunken person?"

"What liking most of this martial art?"

"Give ten Korean commands of tae kwon do— 'Attention!' 'bow!' 'Master!' 'begin class!' 'fight!' 'stop!'

65

'turn around!' 'front up kick!'"

(Strangely, two of the Korean born martial artists couldn't remember some of the Korean words.)

"How tying belt?"

Some of the questions were almost as complicated as the kata. The kata the kata the forms....

Maybe it had something to do with the geometry (or is it trigonometry?) of the forms. How is it possible to start at point A, go from there to C, and then to D, from there to B, from there to F, to E, and back to A?

The kata caused me to talk in my sleep.

"Chester, who is Katherine?"

"I don't know anybody named Katherine."

The kata gave me one-sided headaches. How many steps do you have to take before doing the middle punch, the left forearm block (or is it the right forearm?), the right front snapkick middle punch?

After six years, I was still blanking out on the kata.

I floated up from the sidelines when I heard my name called and began doing all kinds of things. I performed the kata without a hitch.

"Everybody kneel, close eyes, think Nothing."

I sparred with one opponent, two, three. I couldn't see their faces; I couldn't respond to what they were trying to do to me. I was too busy thinking about Nothing and releasing years of pent-up rage, frustration, technique, and energy on them. I'm sure my opponents (who were normally tae kwon do friends) were glad it was over.

"Hey, you were kinda deadly out there," Yong Choi whispered to me when I was finally allowed to be re-seated on the sidelines. I could only smile in reply; my adrenalin was choking me.

Now the squeaking door is slowly opened. Days go by, a week before the first newly awarded black belt appears.

He tries to be casual as he takes his place at the lower end of the front file black belts. He tries to pretend that the belt doesn't really matter all that much and fails. His belt unties itself often, forcing him to turn away from whatever is happening, to re-tie his belt. The belt is stiff and seems heavier than the previous belts.

I go through my paces in a lackadaisical way, anxiously waiting to find out whether I passed or not. Two weeks grind past. I'm getting sick at the stomach from the waiting. I'm going to class every day now, afternoon and evenings, semi-praying for news of any kind.

"Ahh, Mr. Chester, one moment please," the Master's wife sings out to me on my way out after a strenuous afternoon workout.

I'm standing there wondering—what does she want? The Master's wife has never "meant" anything except for the fact that she is the Master's wife, a Queen, the most powerful piece on the board. She floats toward me with this beautiful black belt in her hands. No, it is gorgeous. I have never seen anything as black. It seems to ripple in her hands.

"Long time, not knowing to spell your name in Korean language."

Fuck that, lady! Give it to me! Lemme tie it around my waist, proclaim to the world that I have earned a black belt in Master Kim's hardass dojang, under the dictatorship of a cold-blooded Herman da Silva.

"Thank you," I say, and ease on out. One doesn't bow to the Master's wife. She calls me back.

"You must sign register!"

I ease on back into the dojang. What register? Black belt etiquette is new. What's the deal? Mistress Kim explains: "Register, you sign. All blacka belts, this recorded on roster in Korea from here. Unnerstand?"

Sure, of course, this tells the people who invented the

67

art who is involved and how involved they've become.

I'm stunned to see next to my name "black American."

It's easy to understand the urge to codify—a no designation at all means "white," of course, and "Bi Bim Bap" means Korean, of course, but "black American," nawww, that ain't me.

"Sorry, Miss Kim, I can't sign this."

"Blacka belt register, you sign!" Clearly a hint of future problems to come between the African-American communities and mono-culturalized Koreans.

"I'll have to talk with your husband about this."

I handed the belt (quivering, beautiful, my name in gold thread) back to her. She vehemently refused it—"No, yours. Master this evening." He was *the* Master"; she called him "Master."

I walked home from the dojang feeling confused and a little bit disgusted.

Lady Hilo met me with interesting news.

"We have our passports, and everything else seems to be on track. You still want to go next month?"

"Sure, why not? What's better than October to go anywhere?"

Spain. We had developed a mutually wild hair for Spain. Why Spain? The gypsy stuff, flamenco, the bullfight (that was my idea), the fact that it had been an African colony in Europe (what the hell, I was paying for the trip). She was into the idea of being abroad. What the hell did it matter? It wasn't Okinawa, so?

Lady Hilo was becoming one of my favorite people.

I hadn't reached the point of sincere admiration, however, which provided us with a wholesome emotional balance, because she hadn't either.

"Chester, it's 6:30 PM; did you say you wanted to make the evening session?" I gathered up my uniform, carefully

68

rolling my black belt into a carefully rolled black belt roll, placed my stuff into my gym bag, kissed Lady Hilo ciao, and bungeed to the dojang.

"Mr. Chester, you are not signing? Why?"

Herman was there, translating for three other men that I'd never seen before. They were like setters on the point.

I was pissed and felt disgusted. You mean to tell me, after all the after-class discussions we've had that you think I should be comfortable about signing something that was going to identify me as a lower-case American? I appealed to Herman da Silva for help, and then realized, damn, he's got his own row to hoe. The quick, sloppy look in his eyes told me that he could only translate, not be a strong ally.

"I cannot unnerstand problem!" Master Kim complained.

"The problem, Master Kim," I stated calmly, no need to be excited—I was a "Blacka belt"—"is that I am not a lower-case American, any more than you are a lower case American. I've explained to you, over the course of a couple years, that the so-called Black people in this country are American of African descent. You understand? We are not 'American black' or 'blacks' or any of that.

"I explained to you, six months ago, that we are not representatives or descendants of a place called 'Blackland'; we are Africans who are the descendants of Africans who were imported to America. That makes us African Americans, and that's what I want to see reflected on that register, if I'm going to sign it."

My statement-attitude must've reflected a new militancy or something, judging from the translation-hubbub that lasted for five minutes.

Master Kim slipped back on me, the sly one....

"Other blacka persons sign."

"They were either unaware or historically unsophisticated."

It wasn't a fun number. I felt half guilty about not doing what I was supposed to do. Tae kwon do can put that in you. On the other hand, I didn't feel guilty at all because I was hearing the refrain of a popular Korean song of the day—"We don't know you, don't wanna know you, couldn't care less about you. Dah dah dee dum dum...."

"Master Kim, how many African-American soldiers died to defend South Korea from the communist invasion?"

Another translation flurry. What the hell were they talking about? "Mr. Chester, you don't like 'black' American?"

"No."

"You paying for change to 'African American?'"

"No, I'm not paying for a change. I've always been an African in America. Why should I have to pay to have you correct your mistake?"

Another translation hubble bubble. Herman da Silva: "Master Kim says you should have the belt."

"What about the racial designation change?"

"He'll let you know."

That was it. I was a black belt in a highly ranked Korean tae kwon do dojang that didn't understand that African Americans were African Americans. It would've been easy to predict malevolent happenings at the non-tae kwon do level.

Shit! If Master Kim, an "advanced man" by any degree of calculation, couldn't understand what being an African in America meant (after months of cautious, respectful tutoring), then we'd have to assure ourselves that a Soon Ja Du was just up the road a ways, many Soon Ja Dus and Wha Young Chois.

"Come on, baby, let's get outta here for a minute; let's go to Spain."

"Autumn in New York." What a helluva powerful vehicle is the African-American imagination!

70

I kept thinking that as we walked in and out of the Sloan House, a once reputable "Y" at 34th Street and 9th Avenue.

"Sloan House will be cool for the three days we'll be spending in New York before we board Loftleider to Luxembourg."

How wrong I was. New York in October, "autumn in New York." Who knows? Maybe Charlie Parker's time in New York ("Autumn in New York") might've been spent kicking fallen leaves in Central Park, roasting chestnuts, and such decent stuff as that, but that wasn't the way it was for me and Lady Hilo.

For the three brutal days we spent in Sloan House we fought off "wild dogs" on the elevator to the third floor, simply poked fire into the eyes of the "hyenas" pacing back and forth in front of our room.

The lions-lions were stalking us as we lunged out of Sloan House on a snow-ridden, ice-cold night, heading for the airport. They gave up on us after a few blocks, turned back, their manes and feet frostbitten. We continued our trek, foolish puppies with seven fully loaded valises of dispensable crap.

I remember the blinking looks of other predators as we plodded past. The "cheetahs" and "leopards" couldn't believe that we were what we were until it was too late, and when it got to be vulture time, we were on the Loftleider, sipping cognac en route to Luxembourg.

I often wondered, what good would hapkido and tae kwon do have done us if the predators had struck in New York?

Who knows? My subconscious always answered: maybe it was hapkido and tae kwon do that prevented them from striking.

Luxembourg, Europe. I had been there before and Lady Hilo acted like she had been there before, so there was noth-

71

ing to do but move on. Luxembourg to Paris.

We were going to go deep into things. Paris to Orleans-Lyons-Nimes-Marseille into Spain via Irun.

Irun, Spain, just across the border. A lovely pause in the little hotel; onward. Irun to Madrid. I still don't understand how we made it. We had saddled ourselves with seven huge valises and a couple duffelbag-sized diddy bags. We had decided to spend a couple years in Spain, figuring out what we wanted to do with our lives, mess around a bit, freak out.

"How long do you think thirty-five hundred dollars will last?"

"Shit, if we're careful, we could hang out here for years."

Poor innocent fools we.

We had to jettison a couple of the bags; they were creating wind drags or whatever it's called when you're carrying too much weight. We were on a train in Spain, traveling across a plain; we were freezing our asses off, but we were doing what we thought we wanted to do. The refrain kept popping through my mind—the train in Spain travels mostly on the plain. Our train was oozing across the Castillian plateau, unheated.

"Conductor, how do we turn on the heat?"

"Senor, there is no heat."

An unheated first class compartment on a Spanish train in mid-October is like an unheated ghetto apartment in Chicago on the Westside in January. We shivered and tried to think of stuff to do to warm us up; kissing didn't work, our teeth chattering made that uncomfortable. And going underneath each other's clothes was unthinkable.

"How do Eskimos do it?"

"I don't know, but you can bet it's not on a Spanish train."

Francisco Franco had finally died a few months before

72

our trip. We joked about how long it had taken for him to give up the ghost.

"And now the news!—El Caudillo, El Jefe, Francisco Franco, is still dying. Stay tuned!"

"The news! Spanish dictator, Francisco Franco, is still dying, is almost dead, going, going, not dead yet.... Tune in tomorrow."

"The latest news! Spanish dictator Franco is now almost dead; stay tuned."

We had to stop joking about it after the train conductor peeked in on us with a terrible frown. He had heard "Franco!" and our frozen laughter and was pissed.

Madrid was three hundred kilometers away. America was thousands of miles away, but all over our heads.

"It's got to be the racism; I think that's what I hate the most, the shit that has almost reduced my people to a caste level, that puts a cloud over everything that happens in our country."

The Spanish night slipped past, filled with men in black capes, women wearing mantillas and bright red lipstick. We held unrushed observational conversations.

"Yeahhh, that's a bitch, the racism, no doubt about it. But you know what? Maybe it's just because they're on my mind at the moment..., the thing that bugs me the most, that *has* bugged me the most are the Jehovah's Witnesses."

"Jehovah's Witnesses, huh?"

"They have to be the most insensitive religious group in the country. Remember that Saturday last June when we were making Big Time Love for the first time? You remember?"

We snuggled closer, our eyes glowing with the memory. Lady Hilo was proving to be a delicious package of surprises, great to travel with.

"How could I ever forget? You say we were making 'Big

73

Time Love' for the first time? How about all those other times?"

Clickety clackety clickety clackety—Madrid two hundred kilometers away.

"Those other times were great too, Chester, but this was the first Big Time, you know? I mean, this is when you discovered this little spot inside me, the place that was making cum flow out of me like melting butter."

How could I ever forget it? The sheets on the futon were glued to our asses and backs. The cum seemed to have a perfume to it, never knew cum had an aroma.

"And we look up and there are these two women looking in the window at us, holding up copies of that little magazine they peddle...."

"I said, get away from here; can't you see we're making love?"

"And one of them says, 'Do you know Jesus?'"

"And you said, 'If he can make love like Chester, bring him on in!'"

We cuddled closer and laughed for two miles. We were beginning to have fond memories to share after two years of living together.

"It's a beautiful land, Lady, gorgeous in some places."

"Who you telling? I'm from Hawaii, remember?"

"How could they take a wonderful tool like TV and turn it into a piece of shit?"

"I got some Black militant friends who would tell you, 'It was done to keep poor people of color in intellectual slavery.'"

"Well, it's efficient; you gotta say that. The phones work, most of the time, toilets flush indoors, and food is distributed."

"Terrible food."

"It's better than no food at all."

74

Chapter 7

"The sheer filth of the hypocrisy makes me want to puke every time I think about it. The bullshit about how saintly the Founding Fathers were. The dirty rotten motherfuckers who pushed the original inhabitants aside like excess grass or something. The bastards who locked my people into slavery and then gave us paroles to become serfs, from the plantation to the ghetto."

"We got the right to vote but who can we vote for? If the candidate isn't rich enough to buy some TV time, he's not going to be elected. And if he is rich enough to buy TV time, there's a ninety-nine-percent possibility he won't be the kind of person I'd vote for."

"Yeahhh, it is a kind of strange democracy, isn't it?"

"I'd say it's a *strained* democracy."

"Something's missing, an upper level quality of life is missing. You know what I mean?"

"I'm not sure, Lady; run it down to me."

"I don't quite know how to explain it. It's like a lot of people, even poor people have more stuff than a lot of other people in the world, but it doesn't make anybody feel better. I feel an empty feeling about the way we live in our country; it's full of stuff, but it has no real value."

"America gives you a big headache, if you think about it too hard, all of the stupid contradictions, the weird notions about freedom and justice."

"I love the crazy-quilt mix that we have, racially and culturally. Being from Hawaii really makes me appreciate 'mongrelism.' I love stuff like what we have; the Chinese sausage company that's owned by some Portuguese ladies, managed by Filipinos, with Korean workers. Stuff like that."

"The African people in America, my people, African Americans, fascinate the fuck outta me. We must be the most eclectic people on Earth...."

"Eclec..., what's that?"

"You know, when people become like chameleons, when we can be whatever the situation calls for. We chant, we rant 'n rave, we marry Dixiecrats, fight for the rights of bigots to be bigots, eat Croatian food, create spacecraft, all kinds of shit."

"Chester, what do you think America would've been like if the Founding Fathers had given the Native Americans a chance to act as our social and political role models?"

"It wouldn't've been a perfect society, to be sure, but I don't think we'd be on the verge of extinction, you can bet a fat man on that."

Madrid at 7:30 AM. Brutally cold. No snow, just cold, icy cold. It would be impossible to know what I said to the cab driver to have him drive straight to our room in the Plaza Matute. As a matter of fact, it took us about three days to thaw out. Three quick brandies and two cups of espresso per day helped immensely. The sun came out on the third day and we could really begin to take a serious look at where we were and what was happening.

I got into an immediate love-hate thing with the place. This was the city, the country that had done so much damage to my ancestors, to my heritage, to Africa. I almost envied Lady Hilo; she didn't have to go around thinking: these are the bastards who played a major role in the slave business.

"What the hell, Chester, you couldn't go anywhere in Europe, or Africa either, for that matter, where you wouldn't find descendants of people who had made money selling and buying your people."

Hmmmmmmm....

I must say, the Lady helped me put a bunch of bad vibes into perspective. The weather broke; it was now sunny and warm.

What better way to spend a day than to start it off with a couple cognacs, an espresso, a croissant maybe?

We'd pause in sidewalk cafes to read the papers, people-watch, be watched (the beautiful thing about a sophisticated old city society is that no one stares), have a couple more cognacs, stroll in the park, make leisurely decisions about where we were going to have lunch. Or dinner, if we were going to be out after ten o'clock or so.

"Where do you wanna have dinner tonight, sweet thang?"

"How about that little cafe place, off the Avenida Gutierrez?"

It only took a week to fall in love with a dozen things: the rhythm of the scene (people hurried but no one seemed to be in a rush), cognac and coffee to begin the day (who in the hell came up with bacon and eggs anyway?), the sidewalk cafes, the Prado, the aroma of Cuban cigars (I had to hold the Lady tightly every time one of those suave old

77

birds, the ones with the canes and handmade shoes, strolled past, smoking a Romeo y Julieta), the two-hour afternoon siesta (it makes all the sense in the world; take a damned break please), the way it didn't start happening 'til after 10:00 PM, the Tablao Romero (night after night, the *duende* would come down on somebody 'round about 3:00 AM or so; I think I may have had something to do with it), and the Gypsy brothers and singers who would open their souls for hours, the taste of Jerez de la Frontera (in the place where this beautiful grape is designed), and the Moorish women.

"Chester, look at her; isn't she gorgeous?"

Lady Hilo delighted me with her lack of jealousy. I could never determine if her appreciation of the Spanish women was a way to defuse any attempt (on my part) to do a little adultery or if she was really sincere. I'll have to give her the benefit of the doubt. In any event, she was turning her share of heads too. There weren't many Asian women with Hawaiian waterfalls of gleaming black hair cascading around luscious Polynesian hips, topped by a loving smile, tripping 'round town.

"I saw that dude flirting with you."

"Did you see how well I flirted back? They're obviously not used to us liberated Asian females."

And then, suddenly, it got back cold again.

"Uhh, Senor Duro, why don't you turn on the heat?"

"Hahhahhah, there is no heat, Senor. It will be spring in a few months; it will be warm again."

The memory of the train trip was all the catalyst we needed.

"Shit, if it's this cold now, in mid-October, you can imaging what November, December, and January will be like."

"Why don't we go down south, to the Mediterranean?

78

It'll be warm until January. And even if it gets cold, it won't be like this."

"How do you know?"

"I checked the Spanish Meteorological Bureau."

"Let's go."

We were smarter, better seasoned travelers this trip. We had four bags and two bottles of cognac, destination—Alicante, on the southeast coast.

Alicante is where Chester Himes, the African-American novelist, had lived for a time. Maybe we would run into someone who had known him. I hadn't given tae kwon do a lot of thought for weeks.

"It'll be warm down there; you'll really feel like working out."

"You're right. The idea of taking off my shoes in Retiro Park made my hair stand on end."

Alicante. The sun popped up over the horizon like an orange. We were saved; I could feel it in my bones.

"Baby, you wake?"

"Yes, can you feel the sun?"

"Shit, I am the sun."

Madrid had been the prerequisite for Alicante. Madrid had been the shopping mall; Alicante was a mom 'n pop store. We waded into it as far as we could go.

Within weeks, we had moved out of a perfectly decent Residencia Norte into a fifth-floor ghetto apartment (the home of one Sarafina Sanchez Bou-Gomez and her juvenile delinquent son, Alberto). By mid-November we were members of the community.

Fina was a wonderfully fucked up way to know the real Spain. Spanish; she loved Gypsy music but hated the Gypsies!... "They are a filthy, beggar race and should be chased out of Spain."

The Lady became a Spanish speaker, arguing with Fina;

79

I became a wino. It wasn't difficult to get into that position living with Fina; she could drive you to drink.

"Chester, please bring back two loaves of the two-day-old bread."

"Why not the fresh baked? It only costs a peseta more."

"I like the staleness of the two-day-old, please bring it."

It didn't help matters a lot, either, to have a winery three blocks away. A fifth of excellent sherry cost sixty-five cents. A quart of burgundy that was the color of ink cost thirty-five cents, and Fina, the landlady, drank something called "Tio Pepe" ("Uncle Joe"), a wine that no self respecting Southside wino would even touch. The discipline of tae kwon do drove me to begin working out on the beach (four blocks south) after the second week in town. I ran up and down the mile-long stretch, kicked a bit, performed the kata and returned for my first cognac of the day.

After the cognac at home, a stroll down the cobblestoned streets to my favorite bar for an espresso, another cognac and a look at the daily papers.

"Check this out; America is still trying to make everybody believe it's perfect."

I'd really get into serious drinking 'round about noon; Jumilla was one of my favorite wines, Soberano was one of my favorite brandies, Jerez de la Frontera was my favorite sherry, and if I got desperate, I could sip "Tio Pepe" with Fina.

Alicante was a wonderful place to be intoxicated with, and in. It was a medium-sized Spanish city with very few pretensions. It was supposed to be interested in tourism, but it was quite obvious that they hadn't made any concessions to the trade.

The downtown section made a play for people who wanted Spanish leather, but that was about it. There were no giant hotels overlooking the beach, only a few people spoke

80

English, and the general atmosphere was definitely un-hedonistic. It was a lean, serious, hard-working place where people paid their bills and took their children to the band shell on Sundays to listen to this awful band. Awful.

It was the kind of place that would've bored a lot of people who needed excessive amounts of stimulation. We didn't need that. A loaf of fresh bread (fuck you, Fina), a real jug of wine, a bunch of grapes, a hunk of honest Spanish mortadella, a quarter of goat cheese, a handful of olives, and a balmy afternoon to sprawl out on the Mediterranean fringed beach. What more did we need? Well, we discovered the need for more money after the first month.

"Wowww! You mean we blew fifteen hundred dollars in Madrid?"

"You got that exactly right. Remember all the evenings at the Tablao Romero?"

"I'll never forget them."

We thought about getting jobs but gave up on the idea immediately. The only thing for me was peon-labor and waitressing for her..., if we could get working permits.

"To hell with working; let's just make it on what we got."

Things got tough. I floated around in a wine-brandy-sherry haze until I hooked into the Moroccan hashish dealers (inevitably), adding their product to my dope diet.

Miraculously, I continued working out on the beach every morning. It was late November now and chilly in the mornings. Cognac, wine, brandy, sherry, hashish. I made it a point of honor not to do any of the intoxicants out of sequence.

"Sherry? No, no thank you, it's a bit too early for me."

Lady Hilo got as far as the brandy and stopped. She was painting now and couldn't stop.

"Damn, Miss Lady, I didn't know you could paint."

81

"Sooo?"

She did a stiletto crucifix—Jesus Christ—that went for six thousand pesetas. Fina's sister bought it and made a request for six more.

"Paint six more of these, exactly like that!"

An aside about Fina and her family. The Sanchez Bou family was one of the richest families in town. They owned one (there were two of them) of the bars on the beach, which meant, during the tourist season when the Scandinavians and English flew down on them, they deposited the daily take in trash bags.

Fina, the black sheep, was kept away from the trash bags and given a position in the underground toilet (right behind the bar). It was a miserable position, designed to keep her from damaging "the family name," a recently acquired bit of snobbery that Fina made light of... "Who are we? We were nothing before the war, *nada*! You understand?!"

No matter, I had to side with her sisters after living with Fina for a few weeks. She was a fuckin' loser. The alcoholism was a negative (well, shit, *everybody* was an alcoholic), but that was just one of a series of negatives.

Fina was a study in contradictions. One minute she'd be crying, really crying, about not having enough money to pay her electric bill (kept low, by using a huge magnet), the next minute she'd be buying a chunk of expensive Ghanaian chocolate. She was either weeping or laughing, dying or living, up in arms or down in her cups. The one great thing to be said for her is that she was always Fina, always an individual.

Alberto, her son, was something else. He was a little fascist bastard of the purest kind. He was the one single experimental lab that clearly made me understand the mentality that was responsible for looting the Incan empire, for smashing the heads of Aztec babies against tree trunks and then

82

baptizing them so that their souls wouldn't go to hell, for slavery.

They had a beautiful little dog named "Curro" that Alberto used to try to bend in half, pull out his tongue, stick popsicle sticks in his ass, all sorts of terrible shit. Fina couldn't understand why we'd get upset about the boy torturing the dog.

"He is only a dog; why are you becoming distressed?"

Her oldest sister was even worse than Alberto or Fina.

("Paint six more of these, exactly like that?") End of Aside.

I loved Lady Hilo's reaction to the sister's command (the sister was, incidentally, *La Presidenta* of the Catholic Women's Group. *"La Presidenta!"*)

"Fuck that fat-ass bitch! How dare she tell me what to do?! How *could* I do six more of that piece, exactly the same? That's a one-time work. God! I wish I hadn't sold her that work! What a beast!"

The rain became more frequent and it was chilly, not a Madrid cold, but chilly. Fina would take the *bombone*, a stereo-speaker-sized heater, and glance it away from our freezing knees. It didn't matter a lot to me; I called her behavior "Fina Madness" and kept on drinking and smoking hash. I had also discovered another kind of smoke—cigarettes.

There was this terrible cigarette called "Bizonte" that I developed a Jones for.

"Bizonte, por favor?"

Bizonte, cognac, wine, brandy, sherry, hashish. It began to rain harder; I began to drink my drinks out of sequence.

Sherry, ooppps! Supposed to be cognac now, not sherry.

"Chester, come have a glass of 'Tio Pepe' with me."

We ran out of money in late December.

"What?! What're you talking about? I thought you said

83

we had...uhhh...eight hundred dollars left?"

"We did have eight hundred dollars left, last week; now we have three hundred dollars." I rationalized: what did it matter? The hash was potent, the cognac was mellow, the wine was fine, the brandy was dandy, and I was writing a novel.

"What's the novel about, Chester?"

"It's a composite of Sidney Poitier, Sammy Davis, Jr., and Belafonte, about an African-American movie star, not a black movie star. Dig it?"

It's the custom in Spain to eat a grape for each chime of the New Year—twelve grapes. We knew it was time to leave, popping the grapes for each chime, but we didn't want to. I didn't want to return to the life of an African-American writer in the United States, and Lady Hilo didn't want to return to being a "liberated" Asian woman in the United States, but we knew we had to return.

"Lady, have you had a good time?"

"It's been a blast, Chester, every second of it."

The Bizonte-cognac-wine-brandy-sherry-hashish fog lifted the minute we boarded the plane in Luxembourg.

"Would you care for a glass of wine or a cocktail, sir?"

"No, no thank you."

I couldn't explain the metabolism that rejected the dope after six cold-blooded months of it. The cigarettes were the easiest to dismiss. Who in the fuck wanted to spend the rest of his life sucking smoke into his body?

Lady Hilo had been the big revelation. I studied her Asian profile as she slept across the Atlantic. We had done a real trip together, taken a little money and created a thousand experiences. I felt love, admiration, and respect for her. But I knew it was all over; I felt that. I cried a few times as we crossed the ocean, thinking about us.

"Heyyy, Chester, whassa matter, babe? You got the

84

blues, huh?"

I couldn't tell her how blue my blues were. We were returning to the "Home of the Brave and the Land of the Free," weren't we? That would make any conscious African American blue. Plus those other little psychic bits of cheese that were being fed me. Shit about you, Lady Hilo, for example, I knew; I had seen you deflect the Spanish whip with a glance, turn whole rooms around with a look, stare white women into their place. Be you....

But we were returning to Eraserhead country, and I knew they were going to fuck with you. I could tell when you started straightening out your skirt and brushing your teeth in the seat as we approached LaGuardia.

Yeahhh, I knew why I was crying.

Flash! I almost lost Lady Hilo in Chicago.

"Sure, you can stay at our place"; dear Fred and Lynn, Hyde Park 53rd and University, a beautiful third-floor/ten-room condo. January 1979.

"You OK, Lady?"

"Yeah."

We had taken the bus from downtown, from the Palmer House, to Fred's job at the University of Chicago to pick up the key to their apartment (it was the winter of '79) and now we were walking (ten blocks maybe) from there to the apartment. The baggage was stored downtown; we'd pick that up when we retrieved our Volkswagen from Cousin David.

"You OK?"

I scuffled on for a few steps before realizing that I hadn't heard an affirmative. I hadn't heard anything. I turned around and rushed back to save the Lady from freezing to death. She had paused in the middle of the block with this wise look on her face, her hands glued inside her pockets.

"Keep moving, don't stop! Keep moving goddamit!"

85

It was all so deceptive, the venom of cold (wind chill factor fifty-five degrees below zero), a beautiful powdery snow, the death sentence for the unaware.

We thawed out with ice cubes and Remy Martin. God, what a winter! The train ride from Irun to Madrid was relegated to a warm chapter of the book. In a ten-room house in a well built brick building in Hyde Park, Chicago, United States of Amerikkka, we were forced to huddle around the radiator in the kitchen. It got cold that winter.

Ironically, Lady Hilo and I got closer together and farther apart. I could feel it.

"Chester, what're you gonna do when we get back to California?"

"Same thang I've always done, Lady, pull out my dick 'n rain on folks."

"No, I mean, seriously. What're you going to do to earn a living?"

Uhh oooh…, the "bohemian" had gotten back up into the belly of the beast and become afraid. Or a fool. Or something. I couldn't really figure it out but I felt it happening. We were headed for problems.

But first, the winter in Chicago. We retrieved the Volkswagen from Cousin David, whipped and simpering from maltreatment, and had her re-re-petted and impatiently waited for a break in the ice cap. When did it happen? Who gives a fuck! We got out of there! Maybe it was the first sunny day in February. We were off to the coast, slipping and gliding through Denver. Optimists, we wore sandals and T-shirts inside our VW bubble.

Chapter 8

Back on the coast, in California, blinking at the sun like crazy people, soaking up the juicy rays.

"Now what do we do?"

"Find an apartment and try to get enough money together to get out of here again."

Lady Hilo frowned. It took me a few months to figure out why she had frowned. Meanwhile, we set about the prosaic business of living in the sun again.

She plucked a job out of the newspaper. "Here's something, admissions specialist, Hollywood Presbyterian Hospital."

Hollywood Presbyterian Hospital: "Baby Jane admitted/3AM/ natural father charged with rape of nine-month-old."

"Man admitted/4AM/left foot chopped off/assault."

"Child admitted/4:15/broken ribs, fractured skull, cigarette burns on face and neck/suspected child abuse."

Employment eluded my grasp for a few months; Lady Hilo was becoming a bit strident.

"Chester, what the hell are you going to do with yourself, just sit there and write your life away?!"

"Yes, that's exactly what I'm going to do. I thought you knew that."

We had found a lovely little apartment on Kingswell Avenue, ten blocks from the Greek Theatre, a couple miles from the observatory, going straight up Vermont, north.

We were spared the agony of arguing by my acceptance into a CETA program. Hallelujah!

I cannot recall the mad impulse that drove me to apply for a slot in the program—"Be a legal secretary, earn big bucks!" (This was one of those badly needed, completely worthwhile programs designed to give the poor folks a chance to move into the "mainstream." The program was established, of course, before the United States government became completely hostile to poor people of color, the working poor, the struggling middle class, and all the rest of the people who didn't fit the government's criteria for aid.)

I was knocked to my knees by the acceptance letter from West Los Angeles City College.

"It is our pleasure to inform you that you have been accepted as a student in the CETA program/legal secretary, etc., etc., etc...."

I was knocked out because the whole thing was like a lottery to me, and I had never won anything. Never. This was a gamble that paid off. I was going to learn how to type (a writer should know how), do some shorthand, and get paid for it.

Lady Hilo was enthusiastic... "Wowww! that's great, Chester. Now you'll be able to help pay half of everything."

I attributed her mean-spirited remarks to the ugly pres-

88

sures of working the midnight shift at the hospital. It was much harder to rationalize the motivation for having her hair cut. And she didn't paint anymore.

"What happened to that canvas you were working on, the thing with the scarlet cranes flying in it?"

"C'mon, Chester, get real. Why waste my time painting some fuckin' birds?"

It was happening. We were back in America with a vengeance. She had a job and had to "make it"; a lot depended on her making it. Her family wanted her to "make it," the society we live in wanted her to "make it," and, yes, I think she wanted to "make it" too.

It was clear to me that we were in two different bags; I had it "made" because I had occupied my niche from the age of five, definitely by the time I was eight. I knew who I was, which is infinitely more important than trying to figure out what to do, but are those things you?

In addition, I was watching the change come over Lady Hilo. The bohemian was becoming a conservative (the label doesn't imply that she was swinging from left to right, but rather from an individual to a regimented American. Maybe the hospital had something to do with it), with many of the attitudes that conservatives are known for.

"Chester, you ought to make more of an effort to write for the mainstream, cross over.

"Who is the mainstream-crossover?"

"You know, white people."

"Fuck white people, Lady. Read my shit carefully. I don't even want to write about them, let alone *for* them."

"It's hard to see how you're going to make it with an attitude like that."

We had gone through too much together for her not to be able to speak her mind, but a lot of the shit she said pissed me off highly.

89

"Chester, don't you care if you're famous or not?"

"I am famous."

"Who knows you?"

"All the people who know me."

In addition to the developing conservatism, I checked out the Asian-Americanism surfacing. The Asian-Americanism meant, to me, that she was trying her hardest to be as "American" as possible, that is to say, as white as possible.

"Lady, what's the deal with all these white magazines 'n shit?"

"I like 'em."

"They sure in hell don't seem to like you."

We still had a helluva number going on, but the focus was becoming blurred, going slowly out of focus.

I came up with a different title for them every day: "Four Incredible Sisters"; "CETA Sisters"; "Ladies"; "The Art of the Woman."

Somehow, a bureaucrat somewhere had managed to scratch the covering off of my lucky number and had made me one of the forty-one. I flatter myself by thinking I was just one of the "girls." But I wasn't one of the "girls." I was the only man in the group for the first six months and it got really complicated immediately. The first thing I did (wisely, I felt) when I entered the room and saw these forty necks swivel, was to occupy a seat next to the homeliest sister I could find. (Sorry, Sister X; it had to be you.) I felt like a fox in the henhouse, but I wasn't certain where the exits were, so I thought: chill out, brother, there's plenty to do here.

The other part of the thing is that these weirdly incurable diseases had completely captured my imagination; I wanted some carefully screened living, not a boatload of virused poontang.

It took two weeks for all of us to fall in love with each

other; they were a gorgeous collection of transplanted West African women, most of them from Nickerson Gardens, Jordon Downs, Compton, Main Street, between Century and Slauson. They were brilliant, clever, intelligent, cunning, slick, honest, soulful, interesting, charming, lovely as flowers, ruthless, artistic, uneducated (academically), wise, broadminded, lascivious.

They started breaking through my cool in the third week. Tee Tee took the first shot... "What's the deal, Chester, you gay or somethin'?"

"Uhh, no, I'm not gay. What're you asking me?"

"Hey, we know you gotta be cool 'n everything but we know you dig one of us, which one is it?"

Tee Tee was twenty years old, going on forty, Ethiopian pretty, with these PCP-glazed brown eyes, a wide bow mouth and a totally uninhibited way of moving. I always fantasized about being in bed with her, watching her go from class to class.

"It's you, Tee Tee, it's you."

"Why didn't you say so?"

There, I had done it, I had crashed through the paper wall. They made it easy for me. It became quite obvious to me that they had decided to "harem" me, all of those who were interested in me. I didn't have to go through school-day jealousy scenes, or fight about why I had gone for lunch with this one rather than that one. It's impossible to say why, exactly. I was diplomatic as a man could be; that helped, but, like I said, I think they had decided to "harem" me.

I belonged to everybody, some more than others. The problem I had was to keep everybody slightly in the dark about the depth of my involvement with each of them.

Why lie? I enjoyed the shit out of it.

Tae kwon do? I'd spend a couple days a week jumping

91

around the park, but I couldn't find my way to the dojang. I knew I was going to have to return. What good was a black belt out of context?

But first, there were games to be played with the future legal secretaries of the world.

Chapter 9

TEE TEE

A Figueroa Street motel. Thursday evening, about 6:30 PM, me and Miss Tee Tee sprawled out in a well used bed, staring at ourselves in the mirror above the bed as we talk. We are about five short minutes away from wrapping ourselves around each other.

Tee Tee lights up a joint, passes it to me. It smells like iron being smoked. I take the tiniest toke and pass it back to her.

"Sorry, Tee Tee, I don't smoke PCP."

"Why not?"

"'Cause it doesn't make me feel like I'm high; it makes me feel like I'm crazy."

She sucks in deeply on the joint, her eyes glistening and unfocused. "It makes me feel sexy."

"Oh yeahhh?..." I enjoy the sight of my left hand

fondling her full, firm nut-brown breasts.

"Yeahhh...."

She sucks in again on the joint and reaches under the covers to play with my dick. Her hand is surprisingly soft and gentle.

"Me and Rougenia (pronounced "Row-gin-knee-ah." Why? Who knows?) had a bet on about you, that you had a lotta dick."

I love the look of ecstacy that passes across her face as she caresses my dick. It's obvious that she loves men and their dicks.

"Tee Tee, put the joint out."

She reaches over to scrub it out on the bedside table and turns to face me, her eyes suddenly yellow and green. We kiss with our eyes wide open, caress and feel, progress. She seems to like everything we're doing; I know I do.

"Chester, would you stick your foot in my pussy?"

"Huh?"

"Put your foot, here, put your toes in and wiggle 'em."

"You like that?"

"It makes me cum so good...ooooohh...."

THE SISTERS

I'm half asleep in shorthand, four pages behind in my typing book, and up to my neck in intrigue. Rougenia ("Row-gin-knee-ah") is winking at me from across the aisle.

Wonda, this Samoan-sized woman who wears emerald/paisley/batik/kente-cloth saris to class, passes me a note....

Carlotta is carefully feeling her pussy again. She'll type or do shorthand for a bit, and then as naturally as an animal lover stroking her favorite pet, she'll reach down between her legs and pet it a few times.

94

Never seen anything like it. The way she does it makes it seem totally erotic, but that's because I'm looking at the action out of context. She's just doing what comes naturally. I'm the one who's fucked up.

A few of the sisters are on their periods. It's not so much an odor that tells as an aura. I make a mental note to get a couple dexies from Rosetta (sometimes she spells it Rozetta, Rositta, Roseta, Rosster, depending on how high she is); she has everything.

"Chester, you do 'cane?"

"Coke?"

"Same thing."

"I have."

"Well, I got it if you want it."

And LSD, PCP, dexedrine, psilocybin, peyote, 'ludes, and whatever. Unreal. Shades of Alan Fishe....

IVIDA

"Why you have to use a rubber?"

"It's for protection."

"I've had my tubes tied."

"Ivida, it's for protection against disease, you know?"

"I ain't got nothing, I had a pap smear last month. You clean, ain't you?"

"Look, baby, I'm clean. Yes, I am. I have nothing sexually wrong with me, but that's not the point. Either one of us or both of us could have something we don't know about. I mean, let's face it, germs can hide out and cause you a lot of problems."

"I just don't like rubbers; they take all the good feeling away."

"I don't like rubbers either, but...it's what the program calls for."

95

"You think I got something, don't you? Tell the truth!"

"Ivida, to be honest with you, no. No, I don't think you have anything. I'm sure I don't have anything either, but why take chances?"

"You mean you ain't never fucked a woman without a rubber?"

"Once, years ago...."

"You lyin', Chester, you lyin' yo' ass off."

"What makes you say that?"

"'Cause you are 'n you know it."

"Look, Ivida, I want to make love to you, I really do, but I don't want us to do anything foolish."

"That ain't what you said to Tee Tee."

OLIVIA

"So, what did you do, Olivia?"

"I cussed him and his wife out and tol' 'em they better not never put they hands on my child again. Slant-eyed motherfuckers! They ain't been off the fucking boat but a hot minute and they think they can come into our neighborhoods and do whatever the fuck they think they wanna do.

"Can you imagine?! Where the fuck do you get the nerve to grab somebody's child by the throat? Now I know Latisha ain't no angel, but you come to me when you got a problem with her. She ain't but ten years old and here is this fuckin' grown man gon' grab her by the throat! I went off on their asses!"

"Yeah, I know what you mean. I hate to go in that store. They some of the rudest people I've ever met."

"Disrespectful. We got some of 'em down on the corner from us. Don't nobody like 'em."

I sat at a picnic table in the campus lunch area, listen-

96

ing to a few of the ladies talk about their negative experiences with the recently arrived Korean entrepreneurs in their neighborhoods.

Damn. I couldn't get away from the Koreans, no matter what I did. I sat there, listening, wondering what kind of reception I'd get if I tried to talk about the Koreans to them.

Nawww, they were pissed, they didn't want some kind of socio-historical bullshit shot at them. And what could I say, in any case? The Koreans that I had dealt with were racist, impatient to deal with, poorly prepared by their culture to deal with multi-cultures, but had developed a wonderful martial art called tae kwon do.

VICTORIA

"You know all this is new for me, don't you, Chester?"

"All of what is new for you?"

"This, the cognac in the bar, the seduction scene."

"Victoria, this is no seduction scene...."

"You can be up front with me; the girls have told me all about you."

"What have they told you?"

"About how you've taken them to different restaurants and stuff."

"Ohh, you're talking about my lunch at the Cuban place the other day, with Rougenia, Ivida, Tee Tee, and Wonda."

"Why did you take all four of them?"

"We went dutch, incidentally. Why all four? Because they wanted to go, that's why."

"And what about the evening, me and you here, why did you ask me to have a drink with you?"

Victoria, if I told you the truth, you'd be insulted. How could I *not* ask you out?, the lush bodied, beige colored, gray-eyed old-maid office manager. Such a waste.

"What's the matter, Chester, cat got your tongue? You're not living up to your reputation. Or is it intimidating to have a mature woman sitting across from you for a change?"

"No, you're not intimidating; you're scary."

"I beg your pardon?!"

"Scary, I said scary. I feel scared that you're going to become so romantically paranoid in your old age that you won't be able to appreciate or even deal with a man who wants nothing more than the pleasure of your company."

Very pregnant pause.... "Chester, could I have another one of these? Please, go on, talk to me; I'm not afraid of the truth."

"Uhh, Miss, two more of the same please."

Chapter 10

Slam!

"We regret to inform the students in the legal secretarial group that funding has been cut off, effective..."

Shit. And just when I was beginning to learn where the letters on the keyboard are. And to figure out what the squibbles and slurs in the shorthand book were all about.

It was a cold shot. I freaked out for a minute. I had lost the opportunity to develop new skills, but worse than that, I had lost the little paycheck that came every other week.

"What're you going to do now, Chester?"

I went back to the dojang; that would help me drain off immediately the excess hostility I felt. Master Kim was there, of course, but Herman da Silva was gone. And all of the old-timers that I had kicked around with were gone.

Rumors: "Herman married this white chick, a nurse at Hollywood Presbyterian, and moved to Alaska."

"No, he went to Brazil."

The dojang had a funny feeling for me. I'd go intensely for a couple weeks and lay out for a couple weeks. No one said anything to me. I assume they figured at forty-one years old a black belt oughta have some idea of what he wanted to do.

Lady Hilo was yanging my ass pretty good. And to be fair about it, she was right.

"Chester, what's the deal with you? What're you going to do with yourself? I mean, c'mon! Give me a helping hand here, OK?"

She got so pissed at me she'd start vacuuming the rug under my feet in order to keep me from writing....

I was really down when Alex Haley picked me up.

"Chester, this is your agent; looks like we got a deal going with Alex Haley and Norman Lear. Haley has come up with a show called *Palmerstown*, and he wants you to write one of the episodes; look, how was Spain? Great! I'll fine-tune this and get back to you. My regards to Lady Hilo!"

I stumbled around like a drunk for an hour. My agent? What agent? I had written that part off, cleared my head of the notion that I was going to be given a chance to make any more media money.

Alex Haley, dear man, tried his best to create a reality about two families (Black and white) in a small Tennessee town in the mid-1930s. American television said no thank you, we'll stick with our white sitcoms until the end of the world.

I wrote my episode ("Old Sister"), got well paid, and had the opportunity to tell Alex Haley's partner, Norman Lear, how much I dislike his (A) *Good Times* (in the Chicago projects?!), (B) *All in the Family* (yes, it did make racism seem cute), (C) *The Jeffersons* (gimme a break!).

A small, suave guy with impeccable liberal validations,

100

he smiled and gave me no satisfaction. The *Palmerstown* series went for six episodes.

(I must've done something right; the NAACP gave me an Image award for the episode I wrote.)

I was suddenly struck with the doldrums again.

"Nothing, Chester, nothing. It's a slow season. Got a couple things on the back burner. I'll get back to you."

I went to the dojang mechanically, did my sidekicks methodically, and left.

Lady Hilo and I were getting along quite well. It always seemed to be that way, I noticed, when I had gotten hold of a chunk of change. I couldn't blame her. Who wants to be poor!? Being poor limits your options.

"Lady, why don't we trip down to the bullfight in T.J. this weekend?"

"Chester, let's go see this new play in Westwood."

"Lady, why don't you go shopping?"

"Chester, how about flying up to Frisco and see my sister this weekend?"

The Haley-Lear payoff made life quite pleasant for a few months, but we had had our noses bloodied before; she didn't quit her nasty little job, and I started looking for one.

"Ralph, think you could get me on at Cedars?"

"I saw an opening for a brain surgeon on the bulletin board yesterday; I was thinking about applying for it myself but if you want it...?"

"I'm serious, man."

"I'm serious."

"I'm talking about a job, a j.o.b., anything that would net me a salary every other week."

"Ooohhh, you mean—a job."

"Yeah."

"I'll talk to our mafia-union shop-steward. He'll get you on. It'll be down at the bottom of the pole though."

"I don't give a damn, just so long as I'm making a salary."

Confirmed. A part-time member of the Cedars-Mount Sinai janitorial staff. I wore the vertically striped coat that identified my caste and started stealing the minute I found out where the lobster tails were stored.

Big, rich fuckin' place over there on La Cienega. After my lobster discovery the paycheck became a bonus.

How did I discover the VIP food storage lockers? Just noodlin' around with a trash bag over my shoulder, trying to look efficient. The place was primed for anyone who had an unconventional idea about life, medicine, art, what was considered ethical.

(Ralph, a resident engineer at large, had once donned a white coat, a cap, and a surgical mask and had to stop himself from picking up a knife and slicing into somebody's head.)

It seemed quite right to me that I should take from the rich and sell to the poor. I'm sure there are people in South Central "El-A" who still remember the brother who sold lobster tails for a dollar apiece, chicken breasts for fifty cents each, and filet mignons for a buck. It went on for months. It got scary.

"Chester, what're we going to do with all these lobster tails?"

"Give some of them away!"

"I've already given some away."

"Give some more away!"

It got so good I couldn't believe that I wasn't being set up. Security couldn't be that slack, but it was. I knew why it was the evening I saw a security guard (complete with walkie-talkie) turn a corner with a case of those small bottles of Paul Masson. Corruption is a mother....

I was saved from being caught by a phone call.

102

"Chester, this-is-your-agent, how-ya-doin'-great. Looks-like-we-got-a-goodie-for-you!"

Woww! I was hot! After eight months, more media money. I resolved to spend more time in the dojang.

The Sears Radio Theater saved my financial and spiritual ass for two solid years. For two solid years I was able to write radio scripts that had logic and meat, performed by actors and actresses of intelligence and imagination.

It was a Golden Age for me creatively. I didn't get rich doing thirty-page scripts for less than a grand each, but I wrote something like forty of the bad boys and the experience was devastatingly wonderful.

Westerns, love stories, science fiction, the occult; I wrote 'em all. The producer, a heroic figure in my pantheon, one Elliot Lewis, had one stipulation: "The work should justify our doing it on the air."

SEARS RADIO THEATER
THE ADVENTURE SHOW
ARMANDO PAZ, "EL ENCANTO"

TEASER

HOST

This is_____, and the story we take ourselves into this evening...

MUSIC: LA VIRGEN DE MACARENA (THE MUSIC OF THE BULLFIGHT), UNDER

HOST

...concerns itself with a man's battle with the greatest monster any of us has ever faced, in any arena—his conscience. Armando Paz, bet-

103

ter known to the *aficion* of all the countries of the world as "El Encanto," was and is that man. Before becoming "El Encanto," he was usually called "Armando" or a variety of other names usually used to describe a poor stealer of oranges, or someone who loved the art of bull-fighting so passionately that he would sneak into forbidden pastures and practice surviving their deadly horns on moonless nights. Before Armando was "El Encanto," he was nobody. And he never forgot it.

SOUND: OLES/CROWD MURMURS AT A BULL-FIGHT, UNDER

ARMANDO PAZ
(Introspectively)

E Hey, e hey...torito...come to me. Help me serve them..., you and I. *E hey*, come to me, *torito bravo*.... Help me, if you will, to serve the only monster in this arena.... You and I are the only ones who recognize that the choice is yours. Such great, beautifully formed horns, so well armed by Nature that you only have me to fear, and I am more naturally afraid of you than I am of anything else in the world. *E Hey!*

SOUND: OLES, OUT

ARMANDO

Cowards! They force me to kill you, a profound symbol of freedom and strength, in order for them to experience the idea of death. You are real, they are shadows, screams, moans, fools, creatures who seek out secondhand reality. Yes, the sword sinks into the muscle like butter, and your right horn grazes my groin. We are joined now, in a warm blur, suspended in time for a second, and I feel the vibration of your horn tracing a pattern into my gut. *(Sadly)* I live, your horn dies. The scream of the crowd that forces us to live on each other's blood is the same. Always the same.

SOUND: APPLAUSE/OLES/SEGUE INTO MUSIC: MAIN TITLE. HOLD UNDER. MUSIC IS OUT:

ACT ONE

MUSIC: OVERTURE, THEN UNDER

HOST

Life is not easy; we can't quarrel with that. But how many of us face death each time we go to work?

SOUND: OLES/FADE AS THE RADIO ANNOUNCER BEGINS

ANNOUNCER
(Latin Accent)

Armando Paz, "El Encanto," carved his name into the hearts of the taurine public today. Fighting three magnificent "*cathedrals*" from the ranch of Don Julio Belmonte, he offered his public an incredible display of capework. Those critics who have accused "El Encanto" of being

105

stingy with his capework in the past would not have been able to make that complaint today. He expressed himself superbly in the opening movement by executing those statuesque passes that have justly earned him the nickname "El Encanto" and moved from there to a series of such logically interwoven patterns that they could only be termed extravagant but refined, and above all, terribly elegant....

ARMANDO

Turn that idiot off!

SOUND: CLICK!

MIRA DURAN

What's wrong, Armando; don't you enjoy hearing about yourself anymore?

ARMANDO

I never did, but that isn't something I've ever been able to make you understand.

MIRA

Somehow, according to you, I've never been able to understand a tremendous number of things.

ARMANDO

Please, Mira, let's not argue. Come, sit beside me. I'm tired of fighting.

SOUND: FOOTSTEPS, PILLOWS BEING FLUFFED, OUT

106

MIRA

Why're you so irritable these days?

ARMANDO

I wasn't aware that I was acting any different than...

MIRA

But you are. You were so...so relaxed, so at ease with life when I first met you. I remember thinking...is it possible that this man kills bulls for a living?

ARMANDO

How long was it, Mira? Three years?! Three years is a long time to be "El Encanto."

MIRA

It's your choice; why take it out on me?!

ARMANDO

I'm not taking anything out on you!

MIRA

You are too! You bring your terrible feelings into our relationship and that unnerves me; it makes me feel that I'm not doing something right, that I'm failing you in some way.

ARMANDO

Who could know that better than you?

MIRA
(Pause)

Why do you make these sly remarks, Armando? Haven't I created a lifestyle for us!... Haven't

107

I made your life pleasant?

ARMANDO
(Quickly)

Hah! You think that by surrounding yourself, by surrounding us with all this—all of these things—that some kind of happiness will happen. Sometimes I think that I was happier when I had to steal oranges for a meal.

MIRA
(Exasperated)

What do you want, Armando? I don't understand! The more you have, the less you appreciate it! Or the less you want. What do you want?!

ARMANDO

I want you, Mira.

MIRA
(Purring)

You have me.

ARMANDO

That's not what I mean.

MIRA

So, are we back to this again?

ARMANDO

Is that the way you think about it?

MIRA

Armando, I've told you a thousand times, I will be yours but I will not belong to you. I reserve that privilege for myself. Don't you understand?! I am my own person; I belong to me.

ARMANDO
(Cynically)
That sounds like an odd thing for someone to say who surrendered her so-called "freedom" for a half million pesetas.

MIRA
You're a great one to talk! Think of how much of yourself you "surrendered" this afternoon...for money. How can you...?!

ARMANDO
Think about what it feels like, even the possibility...of being gored in the thigh or in the armpit, the heart...or the eye....

MIRA
(Triumphantly)
For money!

ARMANDO
(Sadly)
No, no, not for money; ...because I have to.

MIRA
I don't understand you when you say things like this. Who forces you to fight bulls?

ARMANDO
I don't know if it would be possible to explain what that means to someone who only thinks in terms of supply and demand.

109

MIRA

Armando, for once, rather than talk to me as though I were a fool, why don't you try to explain? Maybe I *can* understand. You've never bothered to try to make me understand. Who knows? Maybe I'm not quite as dense as you think....

MUSIC: FLAMENCO GUITAR, UNDER

ARMANDO

Mira, place yourself outside of where we are now, outside of this petty conversation....

MIRA
(Petulantly)
This is *not* a petty conversation!

ARMANDO

You asked me to explain something to you. If you want that explanation you must be patient and listen to it.

MIRA

Go...on....

ARMANDO

Good. I must explain to you what I know, what I feel in my own words, because I haven't read the words of other people who write about my art. As a man, I am nothing. *Nada.* I am like other men, but as a creature who confronts death in the shape of a bull many times each season, I am "El Encanto."

                    MIRA
I...I don't quite understand.

                  ARMANDO
I told you that you wouldn't.

                    MIRA
I didn't say that for you to stop.

                  ARMANDO
Should I go on then?

                    MIRA
Yes, of course, go on.

                  ARMANDO
I am a sacrifice, you see, to a spirit in our world
that is older than religion. It is older than my
uncle Juan....

                    MIRA
                  (Laughing)
Is there such a thing?

                  ARMANDO
Yes....

                    MIRA
I didn't mean to...

                  ARMANDO
I understand, Mira, I understand. Pour us some
more wine.

<u>**SOUND: WINE BEING POURED OUT**</u>

                      111

MIRA

There, our best Jerez. Go on....

ARMANDO

I say that I am a sacrifice to a spirit older than
religion. This is true. The spirit is fear, and I
am used by the *aficion*, by the public, to over-
come something that they do not want to con-
front...death. I am the woman who...

MIRA

You are the what...?!

ARMANDO
(Laughing)

I know it sounds incredible but in a way, sym-
bolically, I *am* the "woman" in the pretty
clothes, flirting with a supreme symbol of man-
hood, using the *capote* and *muleta* as fans. And
yet every man in the arena identifies himself
with me.

MIRA

I wish Jose Flores could hear you now.

ARMANDO

Jose knows this already; it is what makes his
aficion so great.

MIRA
(Impatiently)

Yes, yes, I can understand all of this, all of what
you say..., except for the part of you saying that
you are forced to fight the bulls.

112

ARMANDO

But it is true! It is my calling! If I didn't do it, someone else would have to do it, and they probably wouldn't do it half as well.

MIRA

So, you think of yourself as some kind of priest, *ey*?

ARMANDO

I spoke of myself as a sacrifice, not a priest.

MIRA

Hah! You are an incredible man, Armando, incredible! But you wouldn't recognize reality if it gored you between the eyes.

ARMANDO

More wine! I guess it's my turn not to understand you. What are you talking about?

MIRA

I ask you a simple question that only concerns money, and you give me a lot of mystical nonsense about fear, death.... Why can't you make yourself understand that you are giving the public a thrill that they couldn't get in any other way?

ARMANDO

I hope that isn't true.

MIRA

It is true! That is why the Mexicans are willing to pay so much for a *mano a mano* between you and Ramon Garcia. Have you made up your mind? The money will be fantastic.

ARMANDO

Mira, you're hopeless. No matter what we talk about, we always come back to the same thing—money.

MIRA

What else offers so many options?

MUSIC: SWELL TO A CURTAIN

END ACT ONE

ACT TWO

MUSIC: SOMETHING MELANCHOLY/SPAIN OVER-TURE, UNDER

HOST

Going back and forth in time we are quite often able to take mental pictures, emotional glances at our heroes. Especially those of yesterday.

MUSIC: PUNCTUATE, THEN UNDER
SOUND: CAFE SOUNDS, LOW HUBBUB, UNDER

JOSE FLORES

Tell me, Mr. Conrad..., what do you think of the festival this year?

ERNEST CONRAD

I've seen better.

FLORES
(Chuckling)
I like that in you, one who has always seen better. It gives you a great opportunity to avoid dealing with the present and very often the recent past. It offers you a great deal of safety, doesn't it?

CONRAD
Would you say that running in front of the bulls yesterday morning was the way to safety?

FLORES
Please, do not misunderstand, Mr. Conrad...

CONRAD
Please..., Ernest.

FLORES
Ernest, understand me; I do not doubt your courage, only your judgment..., especially when we concern ourselves with the quality of this year's festival as compared to those of past years.

CONRAD
Obviously, the same could be said about matadors.

FLORES
Clearly. *(Calls Out)* Waiter! More shrimp and beer for my *amigo* from America!

CONRAD
I know what you're getting at, *Senor* Flores...

115

FLORES
Please, you may call me Jose.

CONRAD
Jose, I know what you're getting at. Since we occupied this table three days ago, you've been trying to get me to say that Armando Paz was and is, if he were still fighting, the best that ever used the flannel.

FLORES
Perhaps.

SOUND: BEER BOTTLES BEING PLACED ON THE TABLE. OUT/CAFE HUBBUB REMAINS UNDER

CONRAD
Salud!

FLORES
Salud!

(THEY SWALLOW WITH GUSTO. OUT)

CONRAD
Are you saying that I should forget about Manuel Rodriguez? Manolete? Joselito? Cagancho? Procuna, on a good day? Arruza?

FLORES
Well, not completely. But I have to say this honestly.... On a good day, "El Encanto" would have given them all the bath. He was unique, absolutely alone on the face of the planet in his perfection.

CONRAD

With a plate of such excellent shrimp in front of us, *Senor*..., uuh, Jose, I would find it very difficult to disagree too strongly with you. But aren't we forgetting someone?

FLORES

Who?

CONRAD

Ramon Garcia... "Soberano."

FLORES

Oh, him.

CONRAD

It was generally conceded by most knowledgeable *aficionados*, that the *mano a mano* they fought in Mexico was a classic example of a lesser known talent giving the master a taste of the medicine he used to offer.

FLORES
(Coldly)

That's not true. I should know.... I was there. Allow me to take the liberty of giving you the truth. That is, if you were not there yourself?

CONRAD

I wasn't there; I was covering a war at the time.

FLORES

That was unfortunate because you were not present at an event that will always be a part of taurine history. I will tell you what happened.

117

CONRAD

Before you begin. Waiter! Two more of the same, please.

FLORES

As I'm sure you recall, there had been a great deal of agitation from the Garcia people for a *mano a mano*. There were many who believed that "El Encanto" was..., how do you say, "coasting?"

CONRAD

Yes, coasting, taking it easy.

FLORES

I could never agree with that point of view. If you went to the *corrida* and saw Armando Paz, you were present at an event that carried extraordinary emotion. True, he lacked competition, except for Garcia, but he never "coasted...." The bulls would not allow it.

CONRAD

Why was the fight in Mexico?

FLORES

For the usual reason, my friend: money, economics. At any rate, on August 11th..., at four o'clock in the afternoon, on a warm day in the *Plaza Mexico*...

(FADES OUT)

MUSIC: OPENING. LA VIRGEN DE MACARENA. OUT
SOUND: RAUCOUS BULLRING CROWD. UNDER

118

JUAN PELE

(Out of breath from running the bull)
Matador, Armando! Be careful with this one!
He hooks with his left horn...and looks smart
enough to know Latin.

ARMANDO

Run him again, Juan.

JUAN

But...we've already...

ARMANDO
(Angry)
I said...again! Are you the *matador* or am I?!

JUAN

You are, Armando. You are....

SOUND: CAFE NOISES, UNDER

FLORES

There were also a number of disloyal types who
felt that Armando was not only "coasting" but
that he had lost his nerve, the urge to fight the
bulls....

JUAN
(Nostalgically)
He used to ask me, "Juanito, has there ever been
another one like me? Tell me the truth, old
man.... (I guess, at forty, to his twenty, I *did*
seem old). I know you have seen them all. Am
I not unique in this art?" I would have to laugh
at his arrogance and agree. But I always cau-

119

tioned him about making comparisons. Every great *matador* has been a divine manifestation of grace under extreme pressure, deliberately created to purge us ordinary people of certain emotional impurities. They are priests, these men, the ones who do it honestly and with a strong sense of justice.

MUSIC: FLURRY OF GUITAR NOTES. OUT

RAMON GARCIA

My manager..., what a shrewd uncle that one was! He had bribed every major bullfight critic in Spain to promote a fight between "El Encanto" and myself. He had connived and schemed in ways that I would not like to discuss, even at this point in time. He had done whatever was necessary to get me into the ring with "El Encanto." It was not until after Armando made his third *veronica* that it came to me how that pass got its name. A woman named Veronica was supposed to have wiped the sweat from the brow of our Lord on his way to be crucified. Armando, I must admit, seemed to capture some of the tenderness of that moment with his cape. That uncle had *temple*...

FLORES

The bulls were what you would call "flag bulls" in English....

CONRAD

Toros banderos....

120

FLORES

Yes, *toros banderos*, each one as large as this room, armed with horns as wide as your arms spread, faster than a race horse over a short distance, and filled with a violent belief that he was the god of all that his strength and horns could meet.

SOUND: CROWD OLES. OUT

RAMON

The beauty of his movement, the way in which he wrapped himself in his cape as he took his first bull away from the *picador* with *chicuelinas* caused tears to come to my eyes. I knew I would have to search my soul for a new feeling. I knew I would have to offer my life if I wanted to bring honor...and more contracts for next season.

SOUND: OLES. OUT

FLORES

The first one, named "Churro," made a treacherous stab as Armando was making his last pass of the *quite*..., slashing and jabbing with his left horn as Armando went down....

SOUND: HORRIFIED CROWD SCREAMS. OUT
MUSIC: CURTAIN

END ACT TWO

121

ACT THREE

MUSIC: AN OVERTURE, HOLDS UNDER

HOST

Juan Pele, Armando's *peon de confianza*, the oldest and most experienced member of his *caudrilla*, saved him from a serious goring with two bold slaps on the bull's nose. I've never seen a man move toward death with so much courage. Armando rewarded him with a series of *chicuelinas antiguas* that stole the breath from us....

SOUND: OLES, OUT
MUSIC: "DIANAS"/SPONTANEOUS REACTION FROM THE BRASS SECTION, OUT

ARMANDO

It was as though the *pinchazo* that the bull had made was what I needed to bring me back. Back? Back from wondering whether or not I still needed to serve the monstrous appetite of the public. "Churro" informed me, with one quick movement of his head, that it was between us. I thanked him and Juanito with *chicuelinas antiguas*. I cannot really explain the emotion that passed between us, the bull and I. All I can say is that it warned me, made me feel as though I were being used to make a rare kind of love, or music, or something that there are no words for.

MUSIC: GUITAR/TRANSITION/OUT

122

CONRAD

The complaint has always been made...

FLORES

That he was not one to do a three-ring circus full of passes....

CONRAD

Yes, not much beyond the *veronica*, *media veronica*, a few *chicuelinas*, and...

FLORES

Yes, yes, I have heard that. And it was true on this occasion also, but we must make the distinction between the *matador* who only knows a few passes and the master who weaves a spell with a few threads....

SOUND: CROWD CHANTS: "MA-TA-DOR! MA-TA-DOR! MA-TA-DOR!" UNDER

JUAN

My blood turned to fire when they began to scream for Armando to place his own *banderillas*. They knew it was something he never did. But on this occasion he snatched the sticks from my hand, anger showing in his eyes at being asked to do so.

RAMON

The elegance with which he broke the sticks in half on the *barrera*, strolled to the center of the arena as though heaven belonged to him and earth was too dirty for him to place his feet on, is something I shall never forget. You know how critical the Mexican *aficion* can be when they judge the placement of the sticks. I mean, after all, they have "Armillita Chico," "*Carni cerito de Mexico*," Procuna, and Arruza, among others, to look back to. On this Sunday, Armando Paz, "El Encanto," was added to that list. I cannot say more.

MUSIC: "SKETCHES OF SPAIN," UNDER

FLORES

Old men, sitting in the places where bullfighting is discussed...

CONRAD
(Laughing)
Such as this place?

FLORES

Yes, in such places as this, throughout the world, will always speak of those three pairs of *banderillas*. In Mexico, they are called "El Encanto's sticks." "*Los palos de 'El Encanto.'*" He placed one pair standing on the strip that circles the *barrera*. He placed another pair blind, that is to say, he cited the bull for a charge, stood like a statue, and at the last second, faked to his left and dipped the shortened sticks into the bull's neck while looking up at me.

CONRAD

At you!?

FLORES

It seemed that way. It is an emotion that I later

124

discussed with others. They say that they also felt that he was looking at them. I am embarrassed to admit that my eyes were closed and I did not witness the last pair. He cited the bull, turned his back, and, I am told by those who had the strength to watch..., faked the bull to the right side of his body and, as the bull swept under his right armpit, placed the sticks.

CONRAD

That's impossible!

J. FLORES:

Yes, I know. As I said, I couldn't watch. I was so certain that the horn would be slammed into his back.

CONRAD

Waiter! Two more, please.

MUSIC: MELLOW, SEDUCTIVE, UNDER

MIRA

There will always be a number of people who say that I caused Armando to accept the contract for Mexico. It isn't true. It wasn't true then and it still isn't true! He wanted to go to Mexico. He wanted to prove that he was still the best in the world. "What does it matter, Mira," he used to say to me, "if I am not the best in the world all the time?" Those same nasty people who blame me for the Mexican fiasco are the same ones who insist that I ruined him as a man. Of course, that's a lie, too. I don't know why I have to trouble my day with these

things. True, he left me comfortably established, but I think I deserve it.... After all,
think of what I gave up for him.

MUSIC: OUT
SOUND: CROWD SHOUTS "OLE." OUT

ARMANDO

I have to smile, even now, when I think about
the dedication I made to Mira...for the first
bull. Those who were close enough to hear my
words to her could not believe their ears. I
could tell from the shock that their faces registered. I said to her..., "to you, Mira Duran, I
would like to dedicate this noble animal. I
would like to dedicate it to you as a true rep-
resentative of the beast that forces me to fight,
to kill, to bleed, to be unhappy with myself." I
remember the dedication because I had
rehearsed it for two days.

SOUND: BULL SNORTING. OUT
MUSIC: FLAMENCO GUITAR. UNDER

FLORES

There are many words in every language used
to describe certain feelings, certain emotions....
In our language, *duende*..., *pundonor*..., *san-
dunga*..., *temple*... are such words. "El
Encanto" had this...this..., all of it. He opened
his *faena* with four bone-chilling *arrucinas*.

CONRAD

Arrucinas?! I can't remember....

126

FLORES

...the *muleta* held behind the back, offering the bull only a bare strip of cloth as a lure. Most men would feel satisfied to do one, or two at the most. He did four..., completely hair raising... He did many other things this day, with the bull named "Churro." If you may pardon me for becoming poetic about the matter, he revealed the primitive connection between man and beast.

CONRAD

I'm the writer, Jose....

FLORES

I know you are, Ernesto.... I know you are, and for that reason alone I wish you had been there.

SOUND: OLES/CROWD

JUAN

His *faena* was symphonic. I mean that honestly. Many years ago, my father took me to hear the music of a great man; his name was Pablo Casals. I felt the feeling of being overwhelmed in his presence, in the same way that I felt in the arena with Armando that afternoon in Mexico City. With the bull of his life, he created new patterns with his *muleta*. It was a unique marriage, one that will never be seen again. It was not so much a bullfight as it was a dance, but a deadly dance that had all of the possibilities for disaster in each step. "Churro" was one of the great bulls of Armando's life.

127

Only rarely can that be said. He has certain deficiencies in his conduct, such as favoring his left horn, but his nature was clear and he was not ill tempered. What I'm saying, I guess, is that he was a fighting bull from the purest caste, and he offered honor and glory to the man who fought him in a dignified manner. There was something Armando always had—dignity.

SOUND: HOOF BEATS/BULL CHARGING, OUT
MUSIC: FLAMENCO/CANTE HONDO, UNDER

ARMANDO

We were alone in the world, this great, beautiful son of the sons of great bulls. I'd often thought of the intensity that develops between the man and the bull and never fully understood it, not the reason for it or any of that. Not 'til "Churro." The *matador* and the bull must come to know each other more completely than any two beings on earth, within the time span we have with each other, our lives depend on it..., especially the *matador*. This happened with "Churro," in a more special way than it had ever happened before. For a few minutes, as he brushed past my body, I had the feeling that I would never survive. This feeling allowed me to become one with Death. Knowing that each time I offered the *muleta,* and each time "Churro" came for it meant death, gave me the courage to forget about it. Do you understand what I mean? When the presence of it is so strong, it becomes unnecessary to fear it..., it is so close.

128

FLORES

His domination of the bull was masterful. I have seen them all, as you know..., but this was the first time. At one point, as he dropped the bull's head with a left-handed natural and led the bull's face into the folds of the flannel, I had the illusion of seeing a man open a garden gate very, very slowly. And during the course of his movement, as he slowly left this bull poised in one spot with a dazzling *remate*, he would turn to us with a grave expression, as though to say..., "I am doing this for you, I, 'El Encanto,' the only one in the world able to do this."

RAMON
(Agitated)

I hated him; I loved him. I am told that a new record was set in the *Plaza Mexico* for fainting during the course of his *faena*. I found him strange and fascinating to watch. It all seemed to be a dream, the manner in which he led the bull past his body with a series of dreamlike patterns. For long, slow moments, as he moved nearer the horns, I felt as though I were being drawn into a brotherhood, one that only a few men on earth are privileged to join.

MIRA

You would not believe it! The silly women who passed out in the arena..., and it was not too much better on the male side. Yes, of course, he was great! But couldn't they see that he was simply playing on their emotions?

<u>SOUND: FRENZIED OLES, OUT</u>

FLORES

There was this thing that we all understood about Armando, that he hated to kill, which is the function of the...

CONRAD

Matador, killer of bulls....

FLORES

Yes, exactly. We knew this about him. But in some rare way, this reluctance to kill made him a greater killer of bulls.

CONRAD

Ease that one past me again; maybe it's the beer. Waiter!

FLORES

His reluctance to kill made him want to do it and have it done quickly. He was not one to hesitate when the moment arrived.

CONRAD

The moment of truth that becomes an hour for some.

FLORES

But never for Armando. The moment was always a moment.

JUAN

There might not have been more than ten people, if that many, who truly understood why

130

Armando shed tears after he killed "Churro." Knowing him as deeply as I did, I felt that I was one of those.

<u>SOUND: CROWD. OUT</u>

MIRA
It seemed to me that the people around me had gone crazy.

RAMON
"Churro" was an unbelievable experience. I witnessed it, but I didn't believe. I also witnessed Armando's amateurish performance with the two bulls that followed. It was unreal. During the course of his first fight he had been a god. A god, I'm saying! And then...nothing.... He made strange, incomplete motions. His rhythm was odd.... I cannot describe the filth that was screamed at him. The people felt that they were being cheated. He took me from the shade and put me into the sun. I gave Armando Paz the bath.

FLORES
There are those who would say that the last two bulls that "El Encanto" had to face were as great as the first one, "Churro." I would disagree. I would have to say that they were two of the worst examples of what bulls are bred to be that I've ever had the misfortune to watch a *matador* fight.

JUAN P.:
It was really unbelievable, truly. After having

131

done so much with his first bull, one would have to think that he was going to tear up the taurine world with the next two. It was not so.

MIRA

To put it bluntly, Armando blew it in Mexico. After the first bull, he showed all of the signs that the *aficion* needed to believe that he was washed up. I don't know what happened to him. But what does it matter! I'll be accused of causing him to make a poor showing, no matter what! *Es la vida*, no?

<u>MUSIC: CURTAIN</u>

<u>**END ACT THREE**</u>

<u>**ACT FOUR**</u>

<u>MUSIC: OVERTURE. UNDER</u>

HOST
_____ again, with the concluding act of "El Encanto," the story of Armando Paz, *matador*.

<u>SOUND: OUTDOOR CAFE. TRAFFIC NOISES. UNDER</u>

MIRA

Waiter! Two more cognacs here. Hah! They talk about the fight in Mexico. That was nothing! If the truth has a fair face..., he only went to please me, "to earn more money for fancy cars,"

132

as he put it. The fight that the real *aficion* remembers is the one that he staged with himself when he returned.

SOUND: IS OUT
MUSIC: FLAMENCO GUITAR, UNDER

JUAN
He dragged me around with him nightly..., into and out of the lowest clubs of the city. He drank too much..., he...he....

MIRA
It was rumored that he betrayed me with that...that dancer, Teresa Albaicin! If I had found it to be true, I would have clawed her eyes out!

RAMON
Many thought that he had "cut the *coleta*," as we say, you know? Another way of saying that a *matador* has retired.

FLORES
Yes, it is true, I have to admit; I, Jose Bienvida Flores, *aficionado numero uno*, fell into the trap of believing that "El Encanto" was, how shall I say it...?

CONRAD
In a state of remission?

FLORES
Yes, that is one way to say it. In a state of remis-

133

sion 'til the day that an announcement mysteriously appeared on the posts and walls of the city. The announcement was that he, "El Encanto," would stage a one-man fight with the bulls from six of the greatest ranches in Spain. A Miura from Dabrera, a Pablo Romero, a Domecq, one from De Los Gallardo, Vistahermosa, and a Vistavillar. Soccer suddenly seemed much less important than usual.

RAMON

He changed the lives of many of us that afternoon. I have to admit that I went to his *corrida* prepared to see someone who had once been great make a fool of himself. Someone who had become so unsure of himself that he had to fight six superb bulls to show the world that he still had something.

SOUND: MURMURING OF BULLFIGHT CROWD, OUT MUSIC: FLAMENCO GUITAR CONTINUES, UNDER

FLORES

The true *aficion* still pinches himself from time to time, asking himself if such an event ever really occurred. He also ask sometimes..., "Whatever happened to Armando Paz, 'El Encanto?'"

JUAN P.:

I was pleased, to say the least, when Armando pulled himself out of his depression. But, to say that I was pleased with him for arranging a one-man show with *toros* from six of the great

134

ranches in Spain? No, I must admit, I was not pleased.

MIRA

He had to prove himself. What else can I say? After Mexico, after disgracing himself, I think he felt that it was absolutely necessary for him to demonstrate to the bullring world, the only one he really knew, that he was still "El Encanto." I thought it was stupid! There were no guarantees, no contracts. There was not even the possibility of him breaking even!

MUSIC: IS OUT
SOUND: DISTANT PEAL OF CHURCH BELLS PERI-
ODICALLY, UNDER

ARMANDO

They are all mistaken. I had no need to prove myself. Mexico meant nothing to me, nothing! After my *faena* with "Churro," there would not have been anything else. He was the bull of my life. He was also, in some rare ways, the opening of a feeling that I had always concealed from myself.

MIRA

Armando acted..., well, let's say "different" towards me after Mexico. I don't have the words to explain exactly what I mean. I could not reach him. You understand what I'm saying? I could not reach him any longer.

ARMANDO

I made a decision. The decision was to give the

bulls a last chance. There were those who didn't understand. They called my decision arrogance. Or madness. I made my selection from the best ranches because I was the best and I wanted to fight the best, one last time.

SOUND: CHURCH BELLS. OUT
MUSIC: TRUMPET SOLO/LA VIRGEN DEMACARE-NA. UNDER

JUAN

There was a slight breeze moving through the city, but in the arena it was like a hurricane. The worst that could happen on the day of a fight, the wind.

RAMON

As a member of the profession, I tried to question myself, to find out how I would feel under the circumstances. I couldn't. I didn't want to see him gored, or killed, but I did want the public to see him at his worst so that they would know what I felt, that I was the best.

FLORES

The bulls were monsters. There is no other word I could use to properly describe them. Each one was fully grown, well muscled, armed with horns that seemed to have room for cradles in between. They were absolutely magnificent. And he fought each of them with the cold, elegant charm that he was famous for.

CONRAD

Waiter!

FLORES

There was an element of something magical in what he did that afternoon. With the wind and the danger of his cape or his *muleta* misbehaving. There was every possibility that we might witness a tragedy and not a triumph. It was a triumph. He ignored the wind and offered the bulls passes that many said he didn't know..., *pedresinas* on his knees, *molinetes*, *manoletinas*, *afarolados* with the left and right hand, movements with his signature on them. He dedicated each of the bulls to Ramon Garcia and then killed impeccably. The experience was close to being religious.

MIRA

He fought six of the most dangerous bulls in Spain, in the world! And gave all of the money to charity. Can you imagine?! Risking your life for charity?

MUSIC: SWELL TO A CURTAIN

END ACT FOUR

EPILOGUE:

SOUND/MUSIC: CHURCH BELLS TOLL, UNDER

HOST

Each of us has to face life: some only do it in a mirror; Armando Paz did it in his soul. The conclusion of "El Encanto."

137

ARMANDO:
(Nightmare)
No! No! Nooo! Stop! Don't!

SOUND: KNOCK! KNOCK! KNOCK! ON WOODEN DOOR. OUT

PRIEST
(Filtered)
Father! Father Paz! Are you all right?

SOUND: DOOR OPENING. OUT

ARMANDO
(Sleepily)
Yes, yes, I'm all right, Father.

PRIEST
What was it, the bulls again?

ARMANDO
No, it was the crowd again. It's never the bulls that cause me to have nightmares; it's always the crowd, and what a monster it was. I sometimes dream of them charging me, all together.

PRIEST
I understand what you mean, Father. I've been an *aficionado* all my life, and I recognize the beast that you speak of. Shall we go to chapel?

ARMANDO
Yes, I think that is a very good idea. I would like to give thanks for having escaped from the horns of the bulls and the *aficion*.

<u>SOUND: FOOTSTEPS, UNDER</u>

PRIEST

Uhh, Father Paz, I've wanted to ask you...what do you think of this rivalry between Ramon Garcia and Diego Ordonez?

ARMANDO

Well, I would like to say, to begin with, neither of them is as good..., Lord forgive my immodesty, as I was, but... *(Fade Out)* Ramon shows....

<u>MUSIC: FULL TO A CURTAIN HOLD</u>

That's a sample of what I'm talking about. How many African-American writers are allowed to write radio scripts about bullfighting?

I picked up on the radio thing in a number of ways (after all, I had been raised on the radio). I decided to produce a series of shows on the public radio station—KPFK—that would probe the nature of what was happening between the African-American consumers and the Korean entrepreneurs who had moved in on them.

The idea may have been a good one, but the program died after the first show. I thought I knew a little about the Koreans and a whole lot about my own people.

I invited a number of Korean men and women from a cross section of the Korean Directory/business/the arts/middle/upper/lower class.

Six African Americans came: Augustus Stone, the Director of the Paul Robeson Players; Donna Mungen, writer; Mamie Clayton, Western Research Center; Barbara Bell, international lawyer; Al Garrett, researcher; and

139

myself. The Korean community sent Mr. Suhr, an attorney, and Mr. Paik, who taught "Business English" at Southwest College.

I don't think I got two sentences beyond, "Ladies and gentlemen, welcome to this presentation of—African Americans/Koreans, the need for a dialogue...," before the first fight started.

Sister Clayton was severely pissed about the Korean lack of sensitivity to African-American "difficulties"... "I find the Korean entrepreneurs to be as sensitive as a box of rocks."

Mr. Paik, the teacher of "Business English" at Southwest College (a predominantly African-American junior college in South Central Los Angeles), would have benefitted from English lessons taught by Master Kim, even.

Ms. Bell, the international attorney, asked a six-part question that absolutely infuriated Mr. Suhr. He spoke excellent English and he wanted to lecture. "What you people don't understand...."

Gus Stone saved the show from utter chaos. He had been a soldier in Korea and knew how to reconcile differences of opinion. "Well, it seems to me that we have a degree of hostility here that needs to be resolved, or at least diluted, before we can really get into a dialogue.

"As we all know, a dialogue means that we're talking *with* each other, not *at* each other...."

I thanked him for his presence, after the show, and silently promised myself that I wouldn't do that again.

It was obvious, even back then, that African Americans and the Koreans were going to go to the wall against each other. Any sensitive being could see it coming. It would take a few shootings, but the die was cast....

Bam! The Sears Radio Theater closed down. Once again the American exterminators said, "This ain't gonna happen!

140

You people will not be allowed to put quality radio shows on our air waves, no sirree bob!" Bam!

Now what?

"Chester, I'm going to spend a couple weeks with my girlfriend in Diddywhadiddy; when I get back, we're going to have to decide whether or not we're going to continue this relationship or not, OK?"

It seemed reasonable-unreasonable-reasonable-unreasonable-reasonable to me.... "Whatever you say, Lady, whatever you say."

Chapter 11

I returned to the dojang for a few weeks with renewed energy. Peripherally, I could see this short, muscular, brown skinned man with a skullcap haircut, marching up and down the dojang floor, following the cadence of the latest instructor. The mirrors reflect his high frontkick, the forearm block with the left arm, the front snapkick with the right foot, quick left turn, block expected kick, or punch with the right forearm-midsection punch with the right fist.

Punch-kick-block-kee-i! Back to the at-rest position for a minute break. Begin again.

Midway thru the series of punches and kicks I peeled off and stood against the left mirrored wall. I'm not a Korean; I'm not going to become a Korean Bruce Lee; what the fuck am I doing in here?

The class continued as I slowly walked out, bowing to all the proper points and people.

Now what?

Lady Hilo looked absolutely gorgeous to me; she had obviously been swimming a lot: her skin glowed when she swam. We sipped our vino and looked at each other across wonderful moments.

"Well, Chester, what've you decided?"

She crossed her daikon legs and smiled her smile at me. Don't tell me you haven't missed me, you crazy-nut-asshole! I've been gone two weeks, and you don't know where I've been, with my girlfriend in Diddywhadiddy or whatever. So now...?!

"Lady, you know what? I've decided that you did the right thing: you went off with your girlfriend to Diddywhadiddy, and you gave me a chance to think about us for two weeks. And I think you ought to stay wherever you were."

I can close my eyes any time and video her expressions on my mind set. What? We're not going to get back together?! You're going solo? After all I've done for you?! What's going to happen to you, you helpless old fool? Why would you reach a decision like this? Who is she? What's the bitch's name?

"So, this is it, huh?"

"This is what?"

"This is the end of us."

"No, I don't feel like that at all. I think it might be another kind of beginning. You know what I mean? You won't have to worry about whether or not I'm going to be able to face my share of the bills. Number one.

"You won't have to be concerned about whether or not I'm going to live or die. Number two.

"And I won't have you raggin' my ass about how I'm going to make a living, writin' about whatever the fuck I want to write about. No crossover, dig?"

She took it relatively well, I thought. Got vindictive for

144

a moment and sold our jointly owned car to a friend of hers (the girlfriend from Diddywhadiddy), but that was about it.

4616 1/2 Kingswell Avenue. Damn! I was alone for a change. I made a ritual of my daily life; I was not going to go to pieces because the Lady and I had broken up. Nine-thirty AM—workout in Barnsdall Park. Eleven *AM*—shit and shower. Twelve noon—open up the notebook and begin to write, anything, everything.

It was springtime and seemed to remain springtime for years. Flowers bloomed, decayed, re-bloomed. I had contrapuntal dreams, triple-decked affairs that drugged me out of insanely deep sleeps to record them. For the first time in my life (since I was nineteen years old), I was not somebody's husband, father, man, lover, aspiring lover. I was alone, spending days daydreaming.

The fat around my mental middle melted quickly. Suddenly I could smell flowers in the yard next door, from one flight up. My thirst for water overwhelmed me one weekend; I drank until I felt stupid. I could read a newspaper for four hours, a three-hundred-page book in a half hour; it was all relative, as Horacio Wells used to say.

Lady Hilo and I spoke to each other on the phone; there was no reason not to, we weren't enemies.

"Chester, what're you doing?"

"Nothing." Everybody kneel, close eyes, think Nothing.

"Nothing?"

"Nothing."

"Aren't you writing?"

"Oh, yeah, I'm writing."

"Well, isn't that something?"

"I don't really know; is it?"

I sat at the kitchen table, staring at the ivory colored wall of the building next door. I answered the telephone some-

145

times, sometimes I didn't. A number of people stopped popping in on me after I ignored their presence on my doorstep.

"Chester, open up, man, I can see you through the screen door."

"Go away."

Was I going crazy? No, I made that decision early on; I'm not going crazy. I'm just going to do whatever the fuck I want to do for awhile, to see how that feels. The apartment was ideal for my experiment. The front window monitored the approach to my front door (there was no back door), allowing me the luxury of receiving guests or avoiding them.

It didn't really matter because I could ignore them if they arrived unannounced anyway; I frequently did that.

The Jehovah's Witnesses presented another kind of problem (I began to understand Lady Hilo's distress about them), but I soon solved it by appearing naked whenever their persistence became too annoying.

Naked, I ignored my dick for months, even when it stood up between my thighs on sunny mornings and threatened me with impotency if I didn't soak it in Essence d' Pussy immediately.

It was more difficult to ignore the fact that I didn't have any food in the fridge, nor did I have any money. The realization pissed me off. I was going to be forced to get out into the streets, back into all that dripping drama, for the sake of some greens and beans.

"And get me some pussy too," my dick screamed at me as I tripped down the stairs.

It hadn't changed very much since my hiatus. How long was I out of it? Eight months? A year? It didn't matter; I was back in it now with a vengeance.

I was teaching a creative writing class on Sunday mornings in Frances Williams' house. There were twelve to fif-

146

teen serious writers (with the talent to match), and they were giving me a run for my money.

They were the prerequisites for my/our classes in Chino Prison (a bit later), I think.

Weird how shit happens, isn't it? I started teaching writing classes before I had any real idea of how to teach a writing class, way back in 1968, after a bit of time spent in the Watts Writers Workshop.

It was very difficult, teaching a writing class, and also very easy. Number one, if you put yourself into the chair, understanding right off that it's impossible to "teach" somebody how to write, everything's going to be fine, easy. If, however, you come to the front of the class thinking, "By golly! I'll be the one to teach you rascals how to write!" Forget it. Impossible.

I was the non-teaching teacher.

"Class, please listen up, if you want to. Otherwise, fuck it!, just keep on doing whatever you were doing."

All kidding aside, they were a dynamite group and the experience was priceless. Shit, just dealing with Frances Williams was a whole Experience alone.

How old was the sister (circa '78-'79)? Eighty? Seventy-nine? A hundred and two? And too hip. Too hip. She had danced with Katherine Dunham, run around with Paul Robeson, known everybody (knew everybody).

"I was just telling Maya (Angelou) the other day...."

This lady had paid her dues and knew the Hollywood kink so well she had decided to leave it.

"Fuck 'em! It's a bunch of crap anyway."

She had bought herself a piece of land over there on 5th, right off Exposition, and created her scene. The front house was rented, the trailer in the tree-laden back yard was occupied by a succession of homeless artists, and her three-bedroom house was filled with memorabilia of a rich living

147

lifetime.

In addition, she had removed three cars from the adjacent garage and created a fifty-seat theater.

"We must take the *responsibility* for creating our own artistic havens."

Some days she pissed me off; sometimes I loved the shit out of her. I'm sure she felt the same vibes. The workshop clicked. After having locked myself up for so long I felt a juicy kind of freedom happening every Sunday morning that we met to exchange points of view, read our stories to each other, make an effort to be Creative.

"Now then, why don't we start with Myrna...?"

"Why do we have to always start with me?"

"We don't always start with you."

"Well, it seems that way."

"Maybe you're just fantasizing...."

"OK, you win. Here goes.... I call this short story 'A Short Story.'"

The workshop was a critical winner. During the course of the two years we met I can't remember one story, play, article, novel, or whatever that was substandard, not one. I'm sure that the Frances Williams mystique had a lot to do with people doing their best, coming to the sessions with passion and excellence.

"You must take the *responsibility* to be superior!"

And, of course, having been indoctrinated by Margaret Burroughs, Louise Meriwether, John W. Bloch, Jun Bai Lee, Won Chang Lee, Yong Kim, and Herman da Silva, I had high expectations. The writing workshop was the catalyst for the *thought* of returning to tae kwon do. What good is a black belt out of context?

My ambivalence was powered by visits to friends in Compton. I was surprised to hear my most reasonable friends come out with anti-Korean sentiments.

"These motherfuckers have weird attitudes, man, weird."

"Sure, we're not stupid. We know that they are coming to make a profit, that's what business is about, making money. But you don't insult the people you're trying to make your money off of."

"The thing that bugs the hell out of me is that they don't know shit about us...."

"And don't seem to want to know!"

"Their prices are too high!"

"They only hire their own people."

"They're rude. Where is this Asian politeness we've been hearing about all our lives?"

"Why don't they learn how to deal with us as African Americans?"

Capoeira saved me from returning to the dojang.

"Hey, Chester, you still into tae kwon do?"

"Well, uhh, yeah, sort of. I've been chillin' out for most of the year, but I'll be back into the dojang by the end of next month."

"You ought to check this brother who's teaching Capoeira out with me; he just got here from Brazil."

Capoeira Capoeira Capoeira—the African-Brazilian martial art with music and singing, a dance almost.

I was in a state of shocked pleasure. Of course, Capoeira. Why not Capoeira? My martial art! It was the beginning of my own private Brazilian Era.

But first, for my own satisfaction I had to check a few things out. Dojang etiquette had never allowed the kind of behavior to surface that my friends in the CETA program had talked about (remember the sisters in the program?), or the brothers and sisters in Compton rapped about. And my personal experiences had been limited to stray cans of overpriced ghetto beer. I wanted to write about this shit, to get a little deeper into what was happening.

149

The newspapers were only reporting the "big moments": "Korean grocery store owner shot." "Alleged robber shot by Korean grocery store owner."

What would I find if I took a personal survey? Trip through the ghetto 'hoods, stopping in liquor stores owned by Korean merchants, go into gas stations, department stores, wig-cosmetic shops. The "big moments" never seemed to deal with the "small moments," these interpersonal actions that make us people and not snakes or dogs.

"You gon' do what?"

"I'm going into about thirty places over the course of this weekend. I've got a sort of checklist: What kind of service, good, bad, whatever. How people behave, stuff like that."

"Francine! C'mon in here 'n listen to this, Chester is going to spend his whole weekend getting his feelings hurt."

"Well, you know the brother spent a long time gettin' kicked in the head while he was studying that... What's it called, Chester?

"Tae Kwon do, Francine, tae kwon do. And when I bring back my findings, I hope you guys will have an open mind."

"Hey, my mind is wide open. Why don't you start your number off with that little rat-faced motherfucker down the street? The one that's always cussin' under his breath."

"How do you know he's cussin'?"

"You think I've spent a lifetime cussin' and I don't know when a motherfucker is cussin'? Cussin' is the same in any language."

I took the brother's advice and started with the mom 'n pop store in the middle of the block. I had budgeted forty dollars for my socio-experiment.

"I've just checked your fridge and I can't find Heineken dark. Do you stock Heineken dark?"

"No Heineken!"

150

We have a language problem. Does he mean that he doesn't have Heineken dark, or no Heineken at all? No need to push this. He *is* cussing under his breath.

"Thank you."

And Jerry is right, he *is* a little rat-faced motherfucker. Careful now, you're falling into the usual stereotrap that your friends are in, or seem to be in.

Liquor stores, lots of liquor stores in South Central Los Angeles. Many of them owned by Korean immigrants. Wonder where they got the money to buy the liquor stores. Compton Boulevard.... "Good afternoon, my name is Chester Simmons, I'm a writer...."

"No credit, get out!"

"I beg your pardon?"

"Out! Out! Out!"

Well, I'll certainly have to put a naughty mark in front of his name for ill temper. Wonder what made him think I wanted something on credit.

Main Street, I'm tripping around....

"Uhh, pardon me, may I ask you a question?"

"No. No question. You want wine, beer?"

"As a matter of fact, that's what I wanted to ask you a question about."

What an incredibly suspicious look. Maybe the pad and pen are arousing suspicions, but it's too late to put them away now.

"Uhhh, never mind, thank you."

Main Street/Imperial Boulevard.

The woman reaches under the counter as I walk in the store. Does she have a gun? Of course she does.

"Nice day, isn't it?"

A dollar eighty-five for a small orange juice? She literally throws the change on the counter. I know what that's about; it's a cultural thang. Koreans don't like to touch

151

strange hands. I wonder if she knows Black people don't like to have their change flung at them. Yes, flung....

Inglewood, a medium-sized ladies' shop, three aisles. How fuckin' irritating it is to have someone follow you around, bird-dogging every move you make. The saleslady doesn't make an effort to offer help; she just cocks her head suspiciously.

The explanation for her behavior is, of course, obvious. She's been hit by shoplifters and is on guard. But are we all shoplifters?

Another store, still in Inglewood.

"I'm looking for women's panties, the ones with the day of the week on the side. You know, that come in different colors?"

Compound suspicious look.

"Hah hahh ha.... No, they're not for me, they're for my wife."

"We don't have!"

Maybe it's the nature of the sounds in the language. Korean never sounded particularly sweet to my ears in the dojang, not like, say, Japanese or Mandarin Chinese, and, I suspect, when the Korean speaker switches to English, the gutterals sound even harsher.

It's even harsher to hear this English without the benefit of any humor. I've seen Koreans laugh; I've heard jokes in the dojang. Maybe the need to look serious all the time is a protective measure on the "outside."

I need some gas. Alameda and Rosecrans....

"'Scuse me, I'm a stranger in town and I'm looking for...?"

"Three eighty-five."

"Would you happen to know where Burris Street is?"

"Three eighty-five."

"Here you are, and thanks for your help."

I'm beginning to feel anger about the way I feel. Why shouldn't I make myself understand this rudeness? this lack of respect? of intelligent cultural handling? How can you expect to do business with people and not know anything about them? Let me try that one for a change. See what kind of response I get out of that. A fish market in Carson, Samoans come for their twenty-pounders here. Perfect. No customers at the moment.

"I'd like five pounds of the large shrimp. And I'd like to ask you and your husband a question."

She wraps the shrimp; he pauses at the chopping block with a huge knife in his hand; he's gutting a large fish. They wait for my question.

"Uhhh, my question is this: I'm a newspaper reporter and I've been taking a survey of Korean shop owners' attitudes towards their African-American customers. I've gone into twelve stores and I've found an impolite, sometimes rude attitude on the part of the owners. I haven't found that here. Would you like to make a comment about this?"

The man approaches the high counter as the woman obviously translates the blurry question. He explains something to her, for about three long minutes and returns to gutting and slicing.

"My husband say these stupid people, *not* knowing how to act with Blacka customers. They need education-training. Have a good day."

I can't wait 'til the next day to get to Jerry and Francine's place, to give them this positive gem.

"OK, so you started with ratface and went to twenty stores and you come up with one positive out of twenty negatives? Niggahh, pleeeze! What the fuck are you tryin' to do? Defend these assholes!? Chester, let's face it; we got some fucked up shit going on here, real fucked up."

"Jerry, you know something, man, you're right. We do

153

have something real fucked up going on. You know what it is?"

"Run it at me."

"What's fucked up is the fact that we'd continue to patronize businesses run by people who show us no respect."

"Are you saying we should boycott every place that doesn't treat us right?"

"No, Jerry, I'm saying don't shop where you don't feel right. Does that mean boycott? You decide."

The survey ended for a while. It was time to spend a little more time with my writing class and get into a serious thing with Capoeira Regional.

Chapter 12

Capoeira classes in Echo Park; up some stairs behind a sickly green house, a chicken coop off to one side of the gerrymandering yard. The place could be a well-heeled *favela*. Our elevated practice area was once a garage site; bits of metal and nails surface before, during, and after each session.

Two students, Cedric and myself. Henrique is the teacher; the classes are one hour and fifteen minutes long, exactly. After the third lesson I started thinking of us as the "Father" (me), the "Son" (Cedric), and the "Holy Ghost" (Henrique).

Eliana, the "Holy Ghost's" wife, is an element of our Capoeira training. She is pregnant, beautiful, and dominating. Someday she should have a book of her own. I'm sure that when she's ready for it, she'll be certain to tell the writer what to write.

Henrique is an excellent teacher and we are excellent

students. Cedric knows shotokan, and I'm the forty-two-year-old Black black belt in tae kwon do. I am hooked forever after the third lesson. The logic, the rhythm, the movements are sweet to me. Tae kwon do immediately suffers in comparison.

Why have I spent years of my life scuffling and sweating, in pain most of the time, to learn something called tae kwon do? Why wasn't I told about Capoeira?

It was so weird. Here we have this art in Brazil that emphasized music (instrumental: *Berimbau*, *pandiero*, *atabaque*, *agogo*, *reco-reco*, *chekere*) and sheer poetry in a martial art, with a dance step (the *ginga*) that won't quit. An African martial art in Brazil. We felt that. We feel that: The vocal music is mostly in Portuguese (kind of off-brand Africans themselves), but the rhythms are mostly west coast Motherland.

Time flies through the *roda* and we are birds on the wing. We can't wait for classes to begin, we train hard and enjoy every second of it. Back there, behind the sickly greenhouse, Cedric and I quickly acquire the skills to "play" with our teacher; the "games" have started.

Meanwhile, I had to drop the writing class. I made the decision one Sunday morning, taking the measure of the writers in the class. What else could I say to Wendell, Grace, Kay, Janina, Myrna, Percia, and all the rest, after almost two years of saying everything I wanted to say? "This is my last class with you sisters 'n brothers...."

They took my announcement in stride, but I don't think Frances was too pleased. I think she would've preferred firing me.

In any event, I had been pushed out of my ivory tower on Kingswell (to gather up coins for essentials), did the writing class bit, and discovered Capoeira.

I had even given my sex organ a play. Now it was time

156

to return to the nest, arms loaded with greens and beans, to await the next attack of poverty. It didn't take long for it to happen. Damn! You mean to tell me I got to go back out there again?!

"Chester, you want to get together on Wednesday for dinner? Marlene is bringing some of her French pastry."

"Sorry, Lady, Wednesday is a workday-night for me."

"What?! You've got a job?!"

"Yeah, surprise surprise! I'm co-teaching a class with a girlfriend of mine at Chino prison. It's a California Arts Council deal."

I don't know. Somewhere along the way I had thrown an application in the mail, requesting a gig as a creative writing instructor, and my number had come up. The grant was for eighteen months to teach writing at Chino minimum security prison. Weird deal, in a way, to be teaching co-ed in a prison. But that's what we did, month after month.

I think it was the first time many of the inmates had ever seen a Black man and a Black woman peacefully coexist. Or teach. Or do anything.

Donna and I developed the best relationship two different personalities could possibly have, co-leading a writing class. Yes, of course, it's just an idea, a nebulous thought..., but I wonder sometimes if the Artsreach people (the folks who paid us) had thrown us together in that setting in order to perpetrate the negative Black man/Black woman image.

How many classes in writing have you ever gotten into that were taught by two people?

Writing classes, specifically, are not fertile ground for double teaching. Arts 'n crafts maybe, or aerobics, but not writing. Writers are a one-teacher-at-a-time oriented bunch. You can come at them in succession but not vertically. That's what conventional wisdom says....

157

Bullshit. It would be impossible to say how we pulled it off but we did. I think (with all due respect for ego errors made on both sides) that we managed to pull it off because we didn't go into the bit with our hearts hanging out. It was a gig and we were going to do it.

And we did it. On the assigned day, at the proper time, I picked her up or she picked me up, and off we tripped to Chino Prison.

"What're we doing with 'em tonight?"

"Well, they're supposed to have the character sketches to read, remember?"

From this point on I'll have to allow the sister to give her version of it, someday. This is the way it was for me.

Prisons have always been a fact of life for me; somebody was always taking me to see somebody in prison when I was young (my father in Statesville Penitentiary, my mother in the county jail, other relatives and friends), but I managed to evade the corral all my life.

Please understand that that is not an empty boast; it is a loudly screamed fact. I can only attribute the blessings of my ancestors and sheer luck for having escaped the net. I think any Black man in America (aged fifty or so) must be forced to say the same thing.

Chino didn't make me think of Dachau or that notorious joint in Angola, Louisiana, where a brother who had done a bit there told me how they used to cut the grass on the front lawn with their fingernails. And how the guards used to make them kneel and piss in their faces.

"They called it... 'watering' the niggers."

No, this was none of that. It's a minimum security California prison with a standard Black-Brown population. (If you want to find out where the African-American young men are, check out your prison system. Ditto for those interested in Mexican Americans.)

158

It's a bitch going into a prison, even voluntarily, knowing that you're going to come out at the end of your workday.

Physically, it could be a section of Fort Something with barbed wire around it, but that resemblance ends the minute these electronically operated gates begin to open and close behind your ass.

The small hairs used to stand up on the back of my head when we were left in a holding pattern between gates. Damn! What if these motherfuckers have checked into my Cedars-Sinai stealing days? Or gotten hold of some old videos of me ripping off the Broadway store when I was a "stock boy?"

What if they've come across an outstanding warrant?

(I have *no* illusions about the American system of justice. I know that the reason most of the prisons are filled with people of color is because they are *poor* victims of a vicious American system, which gives us the kind of justice reserved for victims of the system who've committed crimes. It's a neat racist trick. If I got a warrant for a traffic ticket, I'd flee to Tibet someplace.)

I could never get ready for entering Chino psychologically (or San Quentin either, or DVI); suddenly, after you've been walked through the metal detector and had your license checked, you're walking on this campus-like walkway into the (in the warmer times, inmates are meeting with their families and loved ones at picnic tables, fifty yards to your left—check out the Latino brother with his hand under his woman's skirt) prison proper.

Enter. The electronic gate clacks open, closes; a guard behind a metal lattice-work checks you out, opens the gate in front of you. You're in a large holding tank; you sign in, go stand in front of another gate. You're in now, all the way. Make a right turn through the handball players doing

159

their stuff against the prison wall.

Politely, they pause to let us through. Never been exposed to such gentility. They almost bow as we pass. We stroll on this narrow path leading to the Education Quadrangle. (Lots of cats around. Gets to be a private joke in my head: well, at least the brothers ain't too far from some natural pussy, if they want to take a chance.)

It's after twilight and the men pumping iron under the lights, to our left, look like ancient mummies.

"Hi ya doin', Miss Lady?" someone calls out.

The flirtatiouness doesn't go beyond that. Maybe that's the code. Who knows? You have to be in prison to be up-to-date with what's happening.

The guard on duty opens the gate to the Education Quadrangle, gives us a room for the class, says a few words, and goes back in the office.

The students come in shortly thereafter. Donna, a lovely brown skinned sister with pretty hips, a gorgeous set of breasts, beautiful lips, eyes, nose, hair, etc., was a drawing card for a minute. But, since she wasn't having any (the word travels lightning fast), these are people who want to get into writing, primarily. I didn't find the inmates hard to relate to or deal with. Well, maybe two that I remember. The only thing I had to do, to keep shit in its proper perspective, was to remind myself that I was the teacher and not the student.

The brothers who came to the writing class had so much to teach me. These were the men who had gotten caught dirty. "Make no mistake about it, my brother, many of us in here are *not* innocent."

They came, week after week, bringing stories that were as gentle as soft summer breezes, as cold and hard as the steel they had used to beat, rob, and kill with. They were not dull, regimented men, and their stories were vivid reflec-

160

tions of their lives. We took smoke breaks together, even though I don't smoke.

"Look, Chester, you seem like a good brother.... I want you to do something for me."

"Is it against the rules?"

"How much are you making per hour for doing this class?"

"What's that got to do with it?"

"Who knows? C'mon, tell me, how much?"

"Twenty-five dollars an hour." That was considered good money to do a class. Of course, it didn't take in wear 'n tear on your car, the ripping of your psyche, etc., etc.

"Twenty-five dollars an hour, huh?"

"That's right; look, we better be gettin' back in, the break is almost over."

"Lemme put it to you straight, I need a little toot right in through there...."

My left nostril immediately twitched, the memory of Hollywood in my spoon....

"What're you askin' me?"

"I'm asking you to bring me an ounce of 'cane.... I'll give you fifteen hundred dollars."

"Whoaaa, you're asking me to bring you a few hundred dollars of cocaine for fifteen hundred dollars?"

"Hey, c'mon brotherman, let's put shit into perspective here. I wanna get high. Money is relative. What good is money gonna do me in here if I can't get what I want? Now here's the way we do this; my woman is gon' get in touch with you.... This is your address and phone number, right?"

It was funny. The inmates weren't supposed to have our telephone numbers and addresses. The inmates weren't supposed to do this or that or a number of things, but they did. The whole scene touched a bunch of nerves in my life. I began to see why the intelligent people would say, "Sending

161

someone to prison is like furthering their criminal education."

I'm not a psychologist or a criminologist, but I could definitely see the truth of that statement in operation. I can easily see that sending more "criminals" (as defined by the American system of justice) to prison is not going to lower the crime rate. The alternative, as simple as it may seem, is to eliminate the inequities of life in America (racism, stomped down capitalism, sexism, anti-humanism, and all of the other negativisms that bog us down, but the people who benefit from this shit ain't about to give it up).

So, we have more prisons, incarcerate more Black and Brown people, escalate the crime rate by educating more people in criminal behavior (if their color entitles them to a jail sentence) and pretend that the "war on crime," the "war on drugs," is being won.

I loved the soft-spoken young Mexican brother who said, "I am not a 'Hispanic,' I am an Aztec prisoner!" who used to write about the "proliferation of the situation."

"Manuel, are you saying that the non-criminal elements in our society are going to be overwhelmed by the criminal elements?"

"That's the way it already is, *hom*. Ain't nobody straight, man. The only difference between me 'n you is that they ain't caught you yet."

"Awright now, Manuel...."

"Hahh hahh hah.... I didn't mean to step on your blue suede shoes or nothin', *hom*. But you know what I'm sayin'. Ain't no fuckin' such thing as 'non-criminal elements in our society.' These so-called 'non-criminal elements' is a bunch of white guys who are sending us to jail for shit that they're doing on another level."

I was dismissed from the program in the nick of time. The brothers had gotten to me so good I was trying to help

162

them plot international robberies.

"If you haven't learned the art of plotting your story properly, then you've been wasting your time robbing poor people like yourselves. The rich people who own the governments are the people with the stuff you want. Here's a simple blueprint, follow it right up to the vault door and blow the motherfucker wide open!"

Yeahhh, they dismissed me just in time. I could see what was missing in the lives of many of the men who were trying to commit crimes against privilege and oppression. They hadn't learned how to plot properly. It was over; the heat simmered, but I wasn't on fire anymore.

The invitation came out of nowhere. The California Arts Council was sponsoring members (past and present) to a three-day retreat-seminar-whatever on this one-million-acre resort-ranch in Solvang. It promised to be big-time bullshit. Donna had another thing to do.

"Chester, are you going?"

"I don't know. I might. I just might go for the hell of it." I had no idea that my life was going to be changed around because I went to the conference for the hell of it.

Beautiful setting, bullshit from beginning. We were assigned living quarters, two or three to a house-cabin, one of those places where a rich couple usually spent the weekend or a couple of weeks, for three hundred dollars a night.

Fireplace, funky redwood, bucolic setting, the whole avocado. It became absolutely clear to me, at our first "all together" session, why I had been invited, why my cabin-house fee had been waived, why it was all bullshit.

How many of us were there? A hundred? Hundred fifty? Out of that number I counted ten African Americans (six women, four men, me included) and maybe six "Latinos" (what a disgraceful fix the Europeans put those people in; "Latinos," "Hispanics," South Americans," "Chicanos," etc.

163

The rest of the artist-teachers-in-prisons covering the State of California were Euro-Americans (oh yes, they had a Native American there too). You know there's got to be something fucked up about a situation like that, where the overwhelming majority of the prisoners are Black-Brown and the artists who are expertising them are white.

It wasn't/isn't difficult to figure out. Despite the fact that America still hates its artists, the racism that permeates the system is still willing to grant their own a major share of the pie, even in prison.

A number of the white artists (bless their souls) talked about this situation in private.

"We gotta make a living too, f' Christ sake!"

They needed us, they needed a few African Americans (males especially, because of the prison demographics) for the color scheme. No wonder they had waived my fees ("one hundred fifty dollars for this, one hundred dollars for that, etc."). The rotten motherfuckers wanted to play with me. OK, let's get into the game; I'm a Capoeirista now, let's git wid it!

"Now then, boys and girls! Let's try to put our itsy bitsy little bitty fingertips on the biggest problem in our society, in our prison system. Daphne?"

"Lack of pottery clay."

"Very good, Daphne. Stephen?"

"Well, I'm dealing mostly with condemned prisoners, you know, guys who've been condemned? And we're having a helluva problem trying to convince them that the watercolors they leave behind are going to be MEANING-FUL. I have a big problem with that."

"Stephen, we have a counseling session set up for you. See Bruce Farmer after this is over. Debbie?"

"Well, you know, it's like this is the first time I've ever been involved in a situation like this, you know? And every

164

time I go into my class, I think...God! wouldn't it be great if we could introduce these guys to Positive Positiveness. I know it really works, because it saved my life. I think that's the biggest problem in our society, the fact that we haven't been exposed to Positive Positiveness. What I think we oughta do...."

"Ife?" Ife Ebun, which means "God's Gift" in the Yoruba language. God! I just love her jewels 'n bracelets 'n that beautiful robe she has on. And how about those dreadddd-locks! Wowww! "Ife, what do you think...?"

"Racism."

"OK, now then, going right along here, Chester Simmons? Chester is one of our African-American male artists-in-the-prisons. Well, he *was* one of our male artists-in-the-prisons before the recent budget cut. Chester, what do you think...?"

"Racism, Timothy, Racism, with a capital R...."

"Jennie, what do you think?"

Ife and I exchanged electric semaphores. What could you expect from a situation like this? We settled back in our lounge chairs, exchanging more signals, practicing African jujitsu-love in the open.

What do you make of this?

It's bullshit.

Why did you come?

Hard to say, think I just wanted to see what they were doing. And besides, it's free.

They gave you a ride too?

They had to, how many Black women do you see here? They needed me for the color scheme.

Me too.

Yeah, you too?

Uhh huh.

We didn't get a chance to interface privately until the

165

following day.

"So, you live up in Oakland, huh?"

"And you're in El-A?"

"Yeah, La La Land."

Oakland. Oakland. Oakland. Oakland had one gigantic memory bank for me. Oakland is the place (somewhere off of University Avenue) where I had gone with my friend Ralph and this beautiful lesbian sister named Judith, years before, to accidentally imbibe a wonderful cup of LSD.

Judith made it wonderful.

"Chester, you OK?"

"I don't know, baby; everything seems to be melting."

"Come upstairs with me."

We went upstairs and made love for twelve hours. I didn't keep track; the people who were bringing us food and water timed the scene.

"Hey, don't you guys wanna come downstairs?"

"Not yet."

"Not yet."

I would never be able to say that I had thrilled Judith to within an inch of her life or anything like that. What I do remember is that she had locked a corner of my brain into the African woman forever.

Ife was a refrain of that song. It was the evening of the end of the bullshit.

"Chester, you ever been to Oakland?"

"Once."

"Aren't you due for another visit?"

"Yes, of course."

"The same invitation is extended to you from me, to La La Land."

"Where can I stay?"

"You can stay with me."

"OK, see you two weeks from today."

I loved that about her, her spontaneousness.

IFE EBUN

"Oh yes, I liked the brother on sight. He was the right size, shape, weight, everything. He even had the right attitude toward the sociopolitical scene. We circled each other for a whole day before we got into anything personal. It's interesting, isn't it, how some people can scope each other immediately. Specially Afrikan people!

I'm not talking about "love at first sight" or anything like that. I think what I'm talking about has a broader range of motion than that.

Yes, of course, I do believe in love, but not in that close order sense of the word that people usually have in mind. My idea of love is freer, more Afrikan....

We're not talking "open marriage" or "killer orgasms" either; we're talking about sharing. I read that in Chester, immediately.

He was a sharing person and he had logic and Afrikanity going for him. I knew something was going to go down.... I could feel it, but I had to know what Wodaabe and Oshun thought of him....

CHESTER

She came, she saw, she bedazzled. I knew she wasn't someone that I could play with. And I had no intention of doing that. The problem I had stemmed from knowing that I had reservations about hooking up with a dyno sister like her.

A smooooth dark chocolate woman, I thought she was a Somalian when I first looked at her in Solvang. A real smooooth textured sister, the ones who think a lot and love

167

to have warm oils massaged into their skins 'n whatnot.

Like I said, she came, she saw, she bedazzled. Three weeks later, I was in her house in Oakland; or to be more precise, I should say, I was in their house.

She co-owned a beautiful house on a hill in Oakland, a four-bedroom house that looked like a small Moorish castle.

I met Wodaabe and Oshun, the sisters who owned the house with her. Wodaabe looked like Ife's sister, but they weren't related, and Oshun was a younger version of Miriam Makeba.

They were an incredibly talented trio; Ife played world class flute, sang in four African languages (was learning Xosa), created poetry on the spot, and danced well enough to be *Ballets Africain* material.

Wodaabe was an ethnomusicologist (teaching Eurocentrically blunt minds at Stanford U.), drummer (conga and kjimbe), painted when the mood was on her, and danced with Ife.

Oshun danced, sang, cooked, and designed Africentric clothes. The house was fermenting. I can't think of a better word to describe the scene. I'd flown up to be with Ife, but I couldn't isolate myself, and she didn't ask me to do that.

I had my room upstairs, but we gathered in the "main room," in front of the fireplace, every night of the week I spent with Ife, to smoke a little herb and rap.

No gin, no beer, no wine, just fruit juice and herb. I lost three pounds and felt real loose.

On the last evening of my stay (I prepared a tofu smorgasbord), after we had settled down in front of the fireplace, the fire and the lights of Oakland sprinkled beneath us...(a little Uzi action here and there, cocaine dogs on the prowl), we lit up a couple Jamaican Blue Mountain joints and started talking about what the deal should be. I was surprised to hear Oshun become so assertive; we were obviously into a place where she felt on top of stuff. Her expression was serious and her words were not spoken in a frivolous manner.

"We think that you should come into this house, Chester; we think that all of us would benefit from your presence, psychologically, spiritually, sensually, artistically...."

What was she saying? Everybody kneel, think Nothing.

Chapter 13

Why should I want to consult my friend Jerry about something as subtle as this? Well, one of the reasons stemmed from the fact that he'd have to consult Francine, who went beyond Dr. Ruth, Dear Abby, Ann Landers, Dr. Joyce Brothers, and all the rest of them.

Sister was keyed "into real." *Is* keyed in. Can read you....

"Now look, Chester, let's get something straight, OK?

"Francine, I just told Jerry and I'm gonna tell you, straight up: I'm asking for your opinion and that's all. I reserve the right to accept or reject whatever, OK?

Francine riffled a sarcastic look in Jerry's direction. He missed it, tuning in to the Discovery Channel.

"OK? Yeah, OK, I'm serious about this shit, Francine. I wanna know what you think."

Jerry, his channel established, leaned back in his favorite cable chair. ("You've gotta get cable, man, that TV, not that commercial bullshit.")

171

"Now look, Chester, don't get me wrong (swear fo' God, the same Uzi fire that interrupted our Oakland conversation interrupted our Compton conversation).... I'm not into multi-anything. OK? Are you receiving loud 'n clear?"

She gripped my neck to press her point home.

"Yeahhh, yeahhh uggh.... I heard you, Francine!"

"Now then, having made that point, lemme say this...."

Uzis and shotguns boomeranged. She paused for a few moments to allow the drug dealers a chance to kill themselves. The deed done, she continued. "Look, pal, these women are into polygamy and you've been chosen to be their husband. Now look, don't get me wrong. If I had been the one to choose a husband for a polygamous household it wouldn't be you. But that's me."

Jerry, finished with the television, nodded in agreement.

"Yeahhh, I gotta agree with Francine, man, you ain't even pulled it off too swell with one woman; how're you gonna do it with wowwwwww! three! Good luck, brother!"

Polygamy? What the fuck were they talking about?

"Francine, Jerry, what're you guys talking about?"

"You know, Chester, don't try to chump us off, you know what the deal is. C'mon now, brother, we know what the deal is. We're from Chi."

I must say this: there was never an awkward moment with us, never. I had met Ife first and got to know Wodaabe and Oshun, in that order. It never varied from that pattern: Ife, Wodaabe, Oshun.

The crucial thing of the whole setup is that we dug each other and we weren't trying to practice traditional West African polygamy. I had not married Ife, Wodaabe, and Oshun in succession, nor had I conducted myself in a traditional way toward their families. Cattle weren't exchanged, relational debts were not incurred; I was not acquiring wives by the usual route. And they weren't off

172

into being the kinds of wives they would've been required to be within the weave of a "traditional" relationship.

"I'm going to be practicing late tonight, so don't wait up!"

We did make a vow, because of the disease thang, that we would be sexually responsible to each other. That meant, because they were all (three) healthy, fully dreaming heterosexual women that they were going to be my sexual partners, period. And vice versa.

We made an appointment and took every sexual test designed by medicine; we four were disease free, and they had all had their tubes tied.

"There are enough Black children without homes already; we can adopt some babies if we want some."

The stage was set. I was going to live with three beautiful, intelligent, talented African-American women in Oakland. I felt that I had died and gone to Heaven.

Marlene and Lady Hilo "did" lunch with me before I left. They were freaked out but supportive.

"Damn, Chester, you must've sharpened up your libido a bit since our time, huh?"

"Sorry Lady, this ain't about libido."

"What is it about, Chester?"

"You really want to know the truth?"

They nodded in tandem.

"I don't really know, on one level. On the other hand, I know that it's something I'm supposed to do; that's why I'm doing it."

"Are you in love with one of these women?"

"I think I'm in love with the idea of being in love with all three of them."

"How do they feel about you?"

"I can't really say; we haven't fully worked that out."

"What do you think you're adding to their lives?"

173

"I'm bringing everything that I am."

They pursed their lips on that one for a minute.

"What's the financial setup; how're you going to handle that?" The kind of question I could expect from Lady Hilo.

"Well, as I understand it right now, they have a common treasury, everybody is responsible for a certain amount each month. I'll join in on that.

"The thing you have to understand is that these sisters have been living together for five years now; they've worked a lot of kinks out."

"Chester, you know what puzzles me most?"

"No, Marlene, I have no idea."

"Why you? I mean, don't get me wrong, it's not that I don't think you're a nice guy 'n all...."

"Marlene, you know something: over the past month I've asked myself that same question and the same answer keeps popping up—why not me?"

We drank a lot of red wine and joked about what I was getting into.

"Marlene, did you know Chester was a big-time polygamist when you guys were together?"

"He was full of adultery; I don't know about the other."

"Chester, why didn't you polygame-ise me and Marlene?"

"OK, Lady...hahh hahhah..., you wanna be funny, huh? Well, just look at us *now*; we've been practicing sequential polygamy, that's all. That's the only difference."

I couldn't really make an argument for polygamy because I didn't have one; I was just going up to Oakland to do my thang, that's all.

We hugged and kissed in the restaurant parking lot.

"You take care of yourself, OK?"

"Write me, Chester; I'll be at the same address until January."

"That's only four months away."

"I know; I'm going to Cuba for a while."

"Anybody we know?"

"You'll know him when the time comes."

I sat in my car for a few minutes after they drove off thinking. It's wonderful to have womenfriends. I was beginning to really look forward to the new adventure.

I was sitting on the plane, waiting for takeoff, before the first attack of anxiety swept over me. What the fuck am I doing? I'm sure I would've jumped out of my seat if I hadn't had my seatbelt on. What the fuck are you doing, Chester? Do you know? The little voice echoed in both ears until the takeoff. Are you going to live with these three women until the day you die? What does the future hold?

I broke into irrational sweats about five or six times, trying to figure out the future.

"Sir, are you all right?"

"Oh, oh yes, I'm fine. I'm fine, thank you. When are we arriving in Oakland?"

"We'll be arriving in approximately fifteen minutes."

I settled back and relaxed.... What the hell, I got thirty-five hundred dollars in my bank account; my health is good; and I'm going to find out something I didn't know.

Ife met me at the airport. She was all smiles, full of beautiful vibes. We kissed. "Wodaabe is doing a class tonight; and Oshun is preparing a little something for us; she thought you might want a little snack when you got in."

The drive to "our" place had a mysterious feel to it. I felt like someone being taken to another planet. A sweet little smile played around the corners of her mouth.

Home. Oshun met me at the front door with a warm hug and a kiss. "Put your stuff away; I'm almost finished with the empanadas."

175

It didn't take very long to discover who the best cook was, and she loved to do it. Her thing was to do lightweight, non-heavy, nutritious things from the African Diaspora. One day it might be empanadas from Venezuela, another day codfish cakes from Jamaica, some kind of shrimp curry from Brazil. By mutual agreement, full-fledged red meat never darkened our door, chicken was seldom served, and for weeks at a time we'd simply have incredibly well prepared salads, curries, fruit, vegetables, goodies.

Back to the first night.

Wodaabe made it in from her class a half hour later; we hugged and kissed.

"You cannot believe how dense these white college students are; a lot of them still believe that Columbus 'discovered' America."

The house was one of those old-fashioned San Francisco types, with high ceilings and a picture window that gave us a sunset and the San Francisco skyline every evening.

Four bedrooms (two upstairs, two downstairs), two toilets, two showers, closet space galore, a ranch-sized kitchen, a half acre of back yard, an earth packed patio on the east side, an attic (and a flat roof, if you wanted to look at the stars), odd little storerooms here and there, spacious.

We nibbled empanadas, sipped fruit juices, and smoked herb as we laughed and talked as though we had known each other all our lives.

I was in love, no doubt about it, with Ife, Wodaabe, and Oshun. I think the key to our success with each other was naturalness. We never got into any kind of message-on-the-bulletin-board kind of stuff, you know, like whose turn is it now?

By 2:00 AM we had made fun of most of the politicians in America and a few overseas, we had exchanged points of view about damned near everything, got emotionally

176

nude a few times.

"I don't give a damn what people think of me."

They were sensitive, kind, civilized, in the John Hendrik Clarke sense of the word: "Industrialization cannot be equated to being civilized; people are civilized when they behave civilly to each other."

The tension was spent; I was tired. I made a shy little wave and eased away from the circle. Ife winked with her off eye. What did that mean?

I took a quick shower and fell between the gleaming white sheets, exhausted. I dozed off with the bronzed images of Ife, Wodaabe, and Oshun in my mind. Beautiful sisters.

Ife woke me up the next morning with a glass of mango juice, her skin glowing, her body covered by a blood red gown. John Coltrane's "My Favorite Things" was playing softly downstairs.

"What time did you all call it a night?"

"Not too long after you. Did you sleep well?"

"Like a baby, baby."

She leaned over and kissed me. I became suddenly conscious that the bedroom door was open. She noticed my discomfort.

"You want me to close the door?"

"Uhh, yes, why don't you?"

She closed the door and opened her gown. An hour later she sprawled beside me, talking about our household.

"You know this is Oshun's idea, don't you?"

"No, I wasn't really aware."

"Kinda strange how it came up. The three of us had just gone through unsuccessful relationships last year; I won't bore you with the details. Just sitting around one afternoon, kickin' it, you know, girl talk, when Oshun started talking like she was in a trance or something. After she finished,

177

we all nodded in agreement: that's what we ought to try...,
a man of our own."

"Don't some people call it polygamy?"

"I suppose so. But this isn't truly polygamy, in the
African sense. We're not sharing each other's families or
anything like that. We're just sharing you, and you're sharing us. It's kind of selfish when you compare it to the real
thing."

They were unusually well thought out on a bunch of stuff
that people were still fumbling with.

"Wodaabe, tell me what you really feel about me. I know
we've only known each other a month but...."

Wodaabe had flaming eyes. Sometimes, when we
sprawled in front of the fireplace her eyes glowed brighter
than the fire. "Chester, I love you with all my heart. I think
you are one of the sweetest, gentlest men I've ever known.
That's how I *feel* about you. I *think*, sometimes, that you
are *one* of the most arrogant, egotistical assholes I've ever
known. That's what I *think*, sometimes."

If you weren't after the truth, it wouldn't pay to ask either
one of them a tricky question.

Something jelled after the first month of my life with
them; we all could feel it.

"Oshun, where is everybody?"

"Ife's in the city with her flute teacher, Wodaabe's in
wringing rednecks at Stanford, and I'm lying up here in
your arms, trying to give you all the pleasure you can
stand."

Oshun was the best cook and the most lascivious. She
was the one apt to lean her big lush pretty butt up against
me in the kitchen, or slip into my bedroom at odd times.

The natural rhythm of what we were doing created a natural rotation. I don't think we were conscious of it; it just
happened.

178

I would wind up spending a week at a time with each of them. When I say "spend a week" at a time, I don't mean we got exclusive or anything. It just meant that whoever was with me during the course of that week was going to be my sexual partner.

It was *very* interesting to see how things patterned themselves. One of my big concerns was how I was going to be affectionate with three women. I don't know, maybe it's because they were so well balanced and disciplined, but that never became a problem. It also may have had a lot to do with how different they were.

Ife was like a cat, she liked to be petted and stroked a lot, but also, like a cat, she was quite independent.

Wodaabe enjoyed stimulating conversation, loved to take long walks on the beach.

Oshun opened up each day with a song and a prayer for all of us. And would fondle my dick like it was a rare jewel or something.

We teased her sometimes: "Oshun's got the hots, Chester; you better lock your door tonight." We didn't have orgies (I'm happy to say), and daily behavior could best be described as "bohemian" but quite circumspect.

Shit opened up for me in Oakland. I don't know whether it was the result of Oshun's daily prayers or the ebo that the Babalowo Ifaymi had me make. But it opened up. Within three to four months of my arrival, I had sold a novel, half a dozen short stories, had been commissioned to write a column about African-American braiding techniques, and was teaching a writing class two hours a week at the East Oakland Development Center.

Ife was doing readings of her work up and down California, playing the flute with prestigious African-American groups, dancing whenever she could, and singing backup on a reggae album.

Wodaabe was on exhibit at the Gallery ("We are the best because we show the best"), creating a new attitude about ethnomusicology at Stanford ("It ain't about so-called 'primitive' instruments, y'all"), and dancing.

Oshun had designed a line of Africentrically oriented children's garments and was negotiating for partnership in a restaurant.

"If they're not open to my touch, forget it."

Oakland was alive with Afrikanity; it was a thread of the weave. I jumped into the whole cloth.

First there was Capoeira Angola with Themba at the Loft on San Pablo. I was beginning to know Oakland and Oakland was beginning to know me.

"Who is the brother?"

"He's a writer, came up from El-A."

I felt I knew a little about Capoeira Regional, but Capoeira Angola was a new ball game. I heard someone call the art the "Father of Capoeira Regional."

Someday we'll have the book that explains the core of all this. For now, let's just say we can date the development of Capoeira Regional, by Mestre Bimba, to 1930-something, and say that Capoeira Angola predates that development by a whole bunch of years. A whole bunch.

Themba had studied with the best Angolieros in Brazil and was dedicated to giving us the finest of what the art offered, him and his best student, brother Raheb.

Once again I felt like the third part of the triangle. We had classes for weeks, only the three of us; Themba, Raheb, and me.

Angola is deep. Physically it's deep, emotionally, spiritually.... I would leave our class some evenings, my thighs screaming from doing the ginga in a squatting position, and drive the wrong way home, knowing that my spiritual antenna was up so high that I really couldn't go the wrong way

180

if I wanted to.

Wodaabe did her best to take me into drumming (the conga, djimbe) but couldn't give me the time I needed.

"Chester, you've got beautiful rhythm but you need to work on your consistency. You know what I mean? You have to become almost a metronome in order to be a really good drummer.

"Why don't you get with Moshe? I hear he's opening up a Kutiro drum class."

Kutiro drum class. Once again I blundered into something I didn't know anything about.

"Yeahhh, you can get in; that'll make six of you altogether."

The kutiro drum ensemble consists of three drums. The drums are tuned by pegs in the sides and come in three sizes; n'dingo is the smallest, next is the ba, and then the cylinder shaped Sabaro, the soloist.

We can oversimplify things (for the sake of brevity) and say that the drums have a language consisting of four words: "Kun" and "ba" with the left hand and "ding" and "da" with the specially designed stick in the right hand. The whole business is, of course, reversed for the southpawed.

Kun ba (left hand) ding da (stick in the right hand)....

The most basic rhythm, of course, would be kun ba ding da, played at a certain tempo. And then it all becomes incredibly complex and logical.

Kun ding da ding da ding da ba...

ba ding kun ba ding kun ba ding kun...

da ding da ding da ding da kun da ding da ding da ding da kun...

Kun ba ding da is being played on the n'dingo, while da ding da ding da ding da kun da ding da ding da ding da kun—or a facsimile—is being played on the ba.

I couldn't use my wildest imagination to try to reproduce the solo language of the Sabaro.

Moshe was a percussion genius and a marvelous teacher. He stroked up, whipped, starved us, put us on bread and water, bullied us, gently led us into the mathematical incredibilities of the Kutiro. I used to leave class sessions feeling enlightened.

Brother Tumani, another genius percussionist, came into my life and took me off into the conga and djimbe. Innocently, I went to him thinking I could get a little mental relief from the demands of Kutiro. After all, I had been semi-playing the conga since my teens.

Tumani turned all those years into a travesty with one simple lesson.

"Funny, I never saw a drummer with two hands only play with one of them."

"Huh?"

"You're only playing with your right hand, did you know that?"

He gave me a new language to study—left right left right left right left right left right left—and then David and Candido came through....

I felt richer than the richest man in the world, and maybe it showed. The brother who had noticed me doing Capoeira Angola movements in the park (and offered an exchange, his tai chi for my Capoeira) spoke to me about it.

"Chester, what's going to happen when one of your ladies decides she wants another way of life, wants to go off with another dude?"

I shrugged. I couldn't even begin to try to explain to him what was happening. I couldn't explain to him that we had already covered that ground. I wasn't being required to play Daddy Moose or Wild Bill the Stallion, trying to keep his herd in line, or anything like that.

We had a beautiful thing going, and the sweeter it got

(over the months), I found myself becoming more lustful. I had never seriously thought of myself as a "great lover," you know, the way some men take pride in that. In some ways my curiosity was always greater than my technique.

It wasn't difficult to notice the change. It took a little longer to figure out the reasons why. I had three women to make love with. If I wanted to be Teutonic about it, I could say: Ife, first week in November; Wodaabe, second week; Oshun, third week; Chester—fourth week.

There was this constant variety of stimulation (I think I became more faceted, by osmotic pressure) and total lack of pressure to perform. Let me explain:

It might be the second week of the month (Wodaabe), but she might be out of town. Or even if she was there, there was no compulsion for us to make each day of our "sexual time" together some kind of job.

"OK Chester, it's Tuesday, second week of the month, let's fuck!"

"Wodaabe, get ready! It's time!"

No, there was no need for anything like that. I mean, number one, all of us were busier than one-armed bandits. Number two, your libido has to be suffering from a real case of low esteem if you don't want to make love once a week.

And we didn't always stick to the normal rotation; that's what I mean about becoming more lustful. One day, for example, under the influence of too much Kutiro, Capoeira Angola, conga drumming, tai chi, and Cuban herb, I tried to surround Wodaabe as she was leaving to teach her class.

She gave me that body loving hug that I grew to love and whispered in my ear, "Chester, I'm running late for my class, Ife's downstairs...."

And to be truthful, they did me like that too. One month we got stuff all twisted around. A wild month that was.

183

Chapter 14

It was the first time in my entire life that I had a chance to live in a completely Africentrically oriented household. It knocked me out. Oshun opened the day with a prayer and a song. There was no self-consciousness about offerings made to our ancestors and the Orisha. We all had ancestral shrines.

We *de*-celebrated most of the usual holidays (we went to the ocean at midnight/New Year's to ask the blessing of Yemanja), Wodaabe was the most merciless of the De-celebrants. She called them "Euro-Hollow Days."

"Why? Why? Why would African Americans gather around a goddamned turkey on a Euro-Hollow Day like 'Thanks-Giving' and ask for the Lord's blessings?

"African Americans?! asking for the Lord to bless them for celebrating the European conquest and genocide of the Native Americans? Baba, give me strength!

"And then, if that ain't bad enough, they throw Christmas

in our faces! I think some of the Europeans became so ashamed of the travesty that they put an X on Christmas.

"Can you imagine what Jesus X would think if he were to walk down State Street on his so-called birthday? People rippin' 'n runnin' around to try to buy their children all kinds of bullshit—bikes, skates, Nintendo games, bullshit.

"What possible connection can you make between a man going out to buy a woman an expensive piece of jewelry on Jesus' birthday? Help us, Baba!

"I ain't through yet! Just so you won't lose all the knack of being bullshitted, in between major HOLLOW DAYS, they fling a bunch of minor HOLLOW DAYS at our heads.

"Negro History..., uhh...sorry, Black, ooopss, wrong again."

"No, Wodaabe, you're right. They've named it 'Black History Month.'"

"Well, I don't even wanna call it 'Black History Month,' even if that's what they call it. I mean, what's supposed to happen during the course of this month that hasn't happened all year?

"They even have us celebrating a slaveowner's birthday during the course of the month—George Washington, the 'Father of Our Country.'"

The sister could be so sarcastic it was like hearing chalk grate on a rusty blackboard.

"And Mother's Day. That's the one that the greeting card company made up. The competition came up with Father's Day.

"There's no need to go on; I'll just stop with July 4th, 'Independence Day.' I'd love to celebrate that one by blowing the White House up with a cherry bomb!"

Aside from serious times, we mostly had good times. Oakland had gotten on to us, and some sections of the population didn't know what to make of our scene.

I had to cuss a couple brothers out who made an attempt to stick their heads into our lives. I was standing at the bar in the Hyatt House, waiting for Ife and Oshun to leave the ladies' room one evening.

"Chester, how you doin', man?"

"You got it, brother."

I was cordial; people were buying my books, strangers spoke to me on the streets.

"Sayyyy, looka here, blood, I wanna ask you something."

Would-be writer? Somebody trying to find an agent or a publisher?

"What is it?"

"How you be doin' what you doin'?"

"What am I doin'?"

"You know, with these three dynamite sisters strung out behind you 'n shit."

By the time Ife and Oshun put in an appearance, I had told the brother all about himself.

"And finally, ignunt ass motherfucker!, it ain't your motherfuckin' business!"

The major league pimp who cornered me in the Great American Music Hall was a bit more subtle. They were having a tribute for Armando Peraza, one of the greatest Afro-Cuban drummers who ever lived. And we had to go.

Strangely, during the course of the year we had been together, we had never gotten out as a quartet. I might make a set with Ife at Yoshis, or check out this master sitar player with Oshun. Sometimes three of us would wind up going somewhere together, to a play or something, but we didn't travel as a quartet, this was a first.

I was literally stunned to see how gorgeous the three sisters were, after everybody got dressed and assembled in the main room for a going-out toke on the Cambodian Red. I was the designated driver; I had a glass of apple juice and sniffed the fumes as hard as I could.

Gorgeous sisters, they looked like tropical birds. Ife liked to play light reds, blues, and yellows up against her skin; Wodaabe tripped on creating face masks; and Oshun, with her dark bamboo brown-yellow self, was partial to white.

All of us were into scents, the more subtle the better. For Oshun, that meant Chanel No. 5. "I don't care if the world buys Opium until it comes to an end; I'm gonna always have me some 5."

"Chanel 5," "Haitian Hips," and "Nzingha" filled the car with lovely vibes. "Mmmmmm..., y'all smell absolutely divine."

The Great American Music Hall in San Francisco. We got there early. "It'll be a drag to get there and have to wait in line."

I don't really think it would've mattered if we had gotten there late, or whatever. We would've gotten the best table in the house anyway.

With Ife, Wodaabe, and Oshun, doors flew open, aisles developed through mobs of people, mysterious hands shielded us from bad vibes; we were a scene that demanded exposure.

All of the drummers were there: Francisco Aguabella, Mongo, Kwasi, Moshe, Candido, David, Tumani....

"Wowww..., this is like looking at drum history."

"Looks like the only people who didn't make it probably have gigs tonight...."

"Or they're dead."

The house was bristling with good vibes, people speaking English, Spanglish, Yoruba, and no English at all. Armando honored us with a visit at our table.

He knew Ife from doing a few gigs with her, he knew Wodaabe, as a visiting lecturer to her ethnomusicology class, Oshun from a party in Chicago, and we knew each other from his days with Cal Tjader when I used to grab a front-row seat and stay there for their two-week engagement. Wherever they played.

I was determined to be there when his hands melted again the way they had melted one night during a number at the Lighthouse in Hermosa Beach.

"Heyyy Chester, my freen', Ife, Wodaabe, Oshun, glad you could make it to this thing." The brother was, as always, infinitely gracious. He had the knack of making the most casual encounter seem special.

"Congratulations, Armando; we're happy to be here for you."

"Thank you; gotta get over here and talk to Mongo.... See you later."

A couple moments in his presence was equivalent to being blessed. We all felt that.

"That man makes me feel so proud, you know what I mean?"

We all nodded at Oshun's statement. Yes, pride, that's what he gave us. We watched him circulating: pausing to have a serious chat with a man who looked like a member of the Addams family, sharing a joke with another, gently shaking hands with someone's grandmother, obviously enjoying this tribute being offered him by his peers and fans.

One by one, "my ladies" tripped away for a moment (the first part of the musical tribute by Machete Ensemble was a half hour away); "Be right back, I gotta get over here and talk to this brother about this rehearsal we're supposed to have on Tuesday evening."

"Be right back."

"Chester, looks like we're holding the fort, huh? Hey Kofi! Kofi! 'Scuse me, be right back!"

I sat there, feeling at ease, royal, if I wanted to use the

bottom line. I was out for an evening with three of the most beautiful women in the country. I was in good health and my creative surge was at its peak.

"Looks like everybody's here, huh?"

The mellifluous voice should've been a tip-off, but what the hell, how do you know...?

"Yeah, everybody's here."

"Mind if I join you for a sec?"

The extravagantly dressed brother slid into the seat beside me before I gave him my permission. My warning system started blinking. Who is this? What does he want? What's he up to? Cocaine dealer was scribbled all over his clothes.

Ife, Wodaabe, and Oshun, total social butterflies when they were in public, were fluttering from one flower to another.

"My name is Dap Sugah Freddy."

I shook hands cautiously with him: you could never tell about brothers like Dap; they've been known to steal the rings.

"I'm Chester...."

"Awww, I know who you are, my brotharrr; just about everybody in Oakland know who you are."

"Oh yeahhhh?"

"Yeah, that's a fack."

We sat there for a few minutes, casually checking out the colorful crowd, the silence weighing heavily between. Come on, Dap, let's get it out of the way.

"Yeah, Chester, my brotharrr, you got quite a rep, quite a rep."

I just stared at him, forcing him to continue his rap about my rep.

"Some folks think you off into a little magic 'n shit, you know what I mean?"

190

I continued my stare; he took it as a green light.

"Like, uhhh, how else could you explain certain things? You know what I mean, my brotharrr? Now, lemme explain what I mean. You see them two black bitches 'n that white girl over there at table number four. Them is my ladies; each one of 'em is a money factory, but I got to keep my foot in they asses every minute of the day 'n night.

"What I noticed about yo' thang is that everybody seems to be so...so free 'n shit; you understand what I'm saying, my brotharrr...?"

I didn't say anything to the brother; I just reached over and clamped my thumb on his windpipe, the way Master Jun Bai Lee had taught me, a thousand classes ago. I squeezed a little to give him an idea of how easy it would be to strangle him to death right there, in the middle of the Great American Music Hall.

I put this crazed look on my face, with the thumb squeeze, and did that rottweiler growl....

I had clamped my hand on his throat like a vise. His eyes bulged a little as he tried to pry my thumb from his throat. I was praying that he didn't have a gun. Only a few people had scoped us, but they were cool.

"Nigger, you crazy! you know that?! crazy!" he spoke in a hoarse voice and stumbled away, back to his table.

Ife was the first to return to the table, and then Oshun and finally Wodaabe.

"Chester," Ife whispered just before Machete kicked in, "I saw that thumbhold you put on 'Paradise Freddy.' Where did you learn that?"

"I know a lot of that shit; we'll get into it as time goes on."

Machete opened us up with a mambo they called "Homage to Armando."

191

IFE EBUN

At first I felt like a traitor for falling in love with this man. What effect was it going to have on our household when I announced that I had fallen in love with Kofi?

I really felt weird about the whole thing, you know? I mean, I was the one who had actually brought Chester into our lives. Sure, it was Oshun who came up with the theory, in a manner of speaking. Oshun had pulled another brother in before Chester but his attitude was wrong. He thought he was supposed to be the Boss. And besides, his spiritual aura was *all* fucked up. We had to dismiss him, quickly.

Chester was perfect. He was considerate, affectionate, not overtly chauvinistic, had lots of smarts, really wanted to create a successfully functioning household with three women. Really wanted to.

And after a couple months of finding out where everything was, he developed into an excellent lover. I hate to admit it now but I did a lot of sneaking around with Kofi, but I didn't break our vow. Kofi was going out of his mind, trying to figure out what I wouldn't tell him.

"Ife, now look, this is driving me crazy. We've been knowing each other for almost four years. We've played music together for three years or so, and you know that I've been in love with you for most of that time.

"You know that, and you're telling me that you love me too, but you won't *make* love with me. I can't figure it out. I'm willing and ready to make a commitment to you.

"If you're afraid that I might have something, let's go get ourselves checked out."

The ambivalence of what I was involved with gave me headaches and heartaches. I loved Chester Simmons. In a way, it would've been impossible not to love him. Maybe it was the fact that he was fifty years old and had spent so much of his life around women, writing about women, loving women, being sensitive to our urges and needs, that made him special.

Sometimes when I'd be feeling low about something, he was the one who had the right word or could stroke my shoulder the right way. No one else could do it.

I loved him but I also wanted another kind of love. Maybe I was after a "private" love. You know what I mean? I didn't have a problem sharing this man with my sisters; that wasn't it.

It was simply that I had fallen in love with Kofi. Just goes to show how fickle the finger of love is, huh?

WODAABE

Before Chester—B.C.—if anyone had tried to convince me that I was going to share a man with two other women, in the same household, I would've laughed in their face.

Me, Wodaabe, formerly..., well, that name and all it represents is dead; but me, a thirty-five-year-old African woman from Besame, Mississippi! Me, in a polygamous setup? No ma'am.

The whole thing had the greatest opportunity for failure with the brother that Oshun pulled in. His aura was *so* funky, I've forgotten his name.

When Ife told us about this brother she had met at this conference I was extremely skeptical. We plotted and planned on the brother; no doubt about that. Ife went down to L.A. to really check him out and brought back a glowing report. I put him under the 'scope when he came for his week's visit.

Chester could make you laugh at yourself because he could laugh at himself. I had a habit of "pontificating," you

193

know the kind of thing that happens to you when you teach school and you get into the habit of teaching all the time.

If your habit gets bad enough, you no longer have conversations; you give speeches. Chester broke me out of that.

"Hold up! Everybody! Quiet! The teacher is going to speak!"

Oshun and Ife had never climbed up on me about this; Chester did, fearlessly. He also knew how to hug me and make me feel important.

The feeling gradually came up in me.... I didn't want to continue to share this brother with these other two women; I wanted him for myself. And I was determined to have what I wanted.

CHESTER

I could almost see the first thread in the cloth unravel, mentally. It was almost that vivid. I think it happened in the third month of the second year we were together, during the third week of that month, when I said to Oshun, "I just can't get enough of you, baby; do you know that?"

We didn't play those games with each other, but I think she knew that I hadn't ever said anything like that to Ife or Wodaabe.

Springtime in Oakland. I seem to be developing some kind of sisterly relationship with Ife; I can tell from the kisses. I'm feeling a bit uneasy about us but, since there's nothing obviously out of sync, I have to go with the flow.

Wodaabe is hot. There's just no other way to put it. She came into my room last night about twelve to get me to help her with a paper she's doing.

We spent about fifteen minutes on the paper and twenty minutes on my bed. Her red eyes got to me; that's all there was to it, her red eyes.

194

Oshun was downstairs singing, rehearsing for a show. I kept praying during the whole time we were having this master fuck that she wouldn't come upstairs. We were into her week.

It was like Oshun was a magnet for me. I couldn't spend five minutes alone with her without wanting to fondle her breasts, or kiss her, or make love to her, or just simply hold her.

Suddenly the tide had turned. I hoped that my feelings weren't that obvious.

OSHUN

It was clearly and simply my fault. I couldn't leave well enough alone. Soon after Chester got up here and I could see that he was *the* one, I started feeding him so many love potions it's a wonder he didn't drop dead. I miscalculated; let that be a lesson for amateurs. I thought my stuff would bring his love down for *us*. It brought it down on *me*.

It was good too; I ain't gonna lie about that, but I didn't want to turn it into a one-on-one thang. I really didn't.

In some ways I dug Chester more in tandem than I did as a solo. Let me explain that a little: you know how it is when you've got a man in your life who has other women? Well, it's not as prevalent now as it used to be, but that actually works better for some people. I mean, who knows? Maybe some of us function better as the "other woman" or as the "other man."

In any case, it seems that things started going downhill right after he picked up this Jones for me. It wasn't like him to become so inconsiderate of our lifestyle.

Ife spaced out, but we found out later that it wasn't totally because of Chester, and Wodaabe almost became a green-eyed monster.

We decided to get together in a "family council" to determine the best way to work this situation out. Needless to say, I stopped doing stuff on Chester long before our meeting.I think he was returning to himself somewhat, but it looked like it was too late....

We called for a "family meeting" on the first of May ("May Day," Wodaabe, "May Day"), because everybody was so busy that it was going to take the last week in April to coordinate our schedules for a 10:00 PM get together.

It would be impossible to capture the mood of the house prior to our meeting. There was a kind of civilized tension, no hostility, but nothing felt right. I decided to ask for a little ceremony to be performed before our meeting, to try for the best outcome of whatever. Everybody agreed.

May 1st, 10:00 PM. I moved a small bowl with water in it to Ife, on my right.... (We were sitting in front of the fireplace in the main room. Oakland seemed unusually quiet for a Friday night.)

"Please wash your hands in this bowl and let us pray that whatever we say will be cool, like this water, and clear, like this water."

After the bowl went around and was returned to me, I asked that we hold hands and "think the most positive thoughts you can think."

I saw a tear in the corner of Ife's right eye. What was she crying about?

We held hands silently for a long time.

"Now, I want to pass this glass of grape juice around for each of us to sip, as a reminder of all the rich times we've shared."

After the glass was returned to me, I got up and placed John Coltrane's "A Love Supreme" on the machine and returned to the meeting.

196

Chapter 15

Oshun opened up with a LuLu. I can still remember how shook I was as she talked. It was a heartfelt, soulful session from beginning to end. "So, as you can see, if it hadn't been for me trying to influence things the way I wanted to influence them, everything would still be all right."

Wodaabe leaned over and hugged her. "No, Oshun, no, I don't believe that. I happen to believe that higher forces govern our activities. Stop me y'all if I start teaching."

We gave her supportive smiles. "Go 'head, Wodaabe, teach."

"Seriously, I do believe that higher forces govern our lives, determine what we should or should not do. As we all know, your ori is here, waiting for you when you get here.

"I think you did what was determined that you should do, Oshun; Chester acted the way he was supposed to act, and a streak of jealousy surfaced in me that I didn't even know I had."

Wodaabe leaned over to kiss me on the mouth. "This is such a sweet, precious brother. He doesn't deserve bad moments."

Ife released a soft flow of fresh tears. "I'm the one who really messed things up. If I hadn't fallen in love with Kofi, everything would still be mellow here."

It was my turn. I felt a tinge of jealousy but I covered it with water from the bowl. "Ife, I don't know who Kofi is, but I do know who you are, and if any man is worthy of your love, nothing can possibly be messed up."

It was a truly interesting hour. It wasn't like anybody had committed a crime or anything, but we felt a great romantic bubble had been popped.

Ife had fallen in love with another man.

"We haven't made love; I wouldn't do that to our house."

I let her know with a look that I was taking her off that hook. We were not going to make love again anyway. Maybe it was the tinge of jealousy in me, but I knew I wouldn't want to make love with a woman who confessed that she was in love with another man.

I could just imagine her whispering in my ear: "Oohh, Kofi," when she really meant to say "Chester."

Ife got to the question before I did. "Wodaabe, why were you feeling jealous about Oshun and Chester?"

Wodaabe stared into the bowl of water for a few minutes before answering. "I think it was social conditioning more than anything; who knows when and how that'll surface? It was obvious that Ife had spaced a bit. Yes, we could tell, sister, we could tell."

They exchanged fives....

"And that suddenly seemed to leave me and Oshun with Chester between us. It was obvious to me that he was favoring her, and as you all know, I am not a good loser.

"My spirit of competition fired up my jealousy. Sorry Chester, Oshun."

I nodded as graciously as I could and stared into the fire.

"Uhhh, I have a little sinsemilla here," Ife cut into the pause. Yeah, why not get high now?

"Chester?"

"Huh?"

"Don't you want to say something?"

I took a pull on the joint and sipped a little grape juice. What was there to say?

"Yeah, I'd like to say a few words." I suddenly had to fight some kind of strange anger down. What was I mad about?

"You'll have to bear with me because I don't have a prepared speech or anything."

They encouraged me with smiles and another hit on one of the joints circling the circle.

"I'll just let it out as it comes. OK? In a way I feel used and betrayed. Understand me now, I'm not talking to anybody; I'm just expressing myself.

"I came up to Oakland with no specific goals, other than to do what I'm going to do for the rest of my natural life...."

"Write!" Oshun spoke out.

"That's right. For the rest of my life. I knew it was going to take a while for us to adjust to the situation we created for ourselves. I was ready to do that.

"The woman who encouraged me to make the move fell in love with another man. The woman who came up with the idea in the beginning was so unsure of how things were going to go, she used some stuff on me. And the other woman *became* a green-eyed monster with fangs."

They looked low, disgusted with themselves.

"But these are minor things, believe me, in the context of all the rest of what's been given me. The three of you

199

have made me feel like a truly blessed man.

"I've shared the warmth and companionship of three of the most beautiful women I will ever know in my life. I feel that.

"Beautiful women start being beautiful from the inside first.... I've had twenty months of Ife, Wodaabe, and Oshun; and, so far as I'm concerned, that makes for the pleasures of a lifetime."

The atmosphere lightened somewhat. How could our spirits get bogged down in the springtime?

I lay in bed that night thinking hard. Ife was gone but Wodaabe and Oshun were still there.

Wodaabe had turned jealous, and I didn't ever feel that I'd be able to trust Oshun again. I felt the only solution for me was to go back to where I came from. Or move onward to Ghana, where I had been threatening to go for a number of years.

I decided to let the dust settle before I got into the serious planning stage.

It took about two weeks for me to make the decision....

"Wodaabe, Oshun, I'm going back to L.A."

They made halfhearted attempts to talk me out of it, but we all knew that something had been broken that we'd never be able to put back together again.

"This is a big house; what're we going to do with ourselves in here?"

"All you need to do is put a notice on the University bulletin board—'two homeowners need paying roommates'—you'd have a line up at your front door."

Once my decision had been made, I moved quickly.

"I'll be leaving on Friday...."

"This coming Friday?"

"This coming Friday."

200

We had a pretty intense week. Ife came over; we sat out in the patio and rapped.

"Chester, how do you feel? Do you feel that you've been a part of something that failed?"

"No, not really. I just feel that the force of circumstances has determined something I don't have any control over."

"Why do you have to go back down to L.A.; why don't you stay here in Oakland?"

I had thought about that for hours, but I had to veto the idea. Somehow, I just couldn't see myself in the same place with Ife, Wodaabe, and Oshun.

Oakland is a tight little place and we were bound to be tripping all over each other. I didn't want that. And besides, I found myself missing the orange trees and sunshine of Southern California.

"Ife, I thought about staying up here, but I don't think it would be too cool. You know what I mean?"

Yeah, it was a pretty intense week. Oshun came up with this herb from Thailand that put us on another plane.

"So this is what thai stick is, huh?"

"Yeahhh, it's something else, ain't it?"

I think we burned more incense, played more music (recorded and live), meditated, ate more delicious food ("Oshun, you don't have any secret ingredients in here, do you, baby?"), and talked more than we had ever talked in all the time we had been together.

Ife slid in on Thursday afternoon, "did" lunch with us, and gave me a beautiful red-black-and-green ileke.

"It's been blessed; I hope it's lucky for you," she said as she put it over my head.

"Thank you, Ife; you've blessed me by giving it to me."

She kissed me and left.

Thursday night about 10:30 PM, Wodaabe, Oshun, and I had spent a lovely afternoon and evening together, no bad

201

vibes, no sadness, just lovely.

"I'm going to miss all of you; you know that?"

"We're going to miss you too, Chester."

Later, I went upstairs to pack, my mind drifting....

A half hour later Oshun called to me from the main room downstairs. I loved the way she sang my name.

"Chhheeessssteeeer! Come down here a moment; we have something for you."

I tripped down, not thinking anything special. The sight of the two of them standing in a wide circle of candles blew my mind. They were naked and gleaming with lush smelling oils; Oshun crooked her finger at me to join them.

"We want to give you something to remember us by."

It took me about ten seconds to strip and join them in the circle of candles, a couple mattress sized futons on the floor in front of the fireplace.

We had never gone the orgy route and, as a matter of feeling, this wasn't an orgy either; I had the feeling that something sacred was happening, rather than something profane.

Charlie Parker, Miles, Diz, Tatum, Ornette, Johnny Hartsman, Billie, Sarah, Dinah, Bud, Monk, and a bunch of others spilled out on us from tapes as we loved each other. Old-time music for old-time loving....

The sun was peeking up at us over the San Francisco skyline as I slid off of Wodaabe's back and kissed them both....

"Good night..., uhh, good morning."

We slept 'til noon. My flight was scheduled for 2:00 PM.

We hugged and kissed and cried like babies at the airport, confusing a few people. Our kisses weren't brother-sister type kisses, and I kept going from one to the other.

"Chester, don't forget us, OK?"

202

"I'll write you. And the phone works."

"Will you come back to see us?"

"As often as possible."

Ife ran up from out of nowhere, and then we really got sticky. I had a small audience by the time I got in the line to get on board.

"We love you, Chester; don't forget that!"

"I love you too."

I settled into my seat, fastened the seat belt, feeling calm and happy.

The short time that it takes for the plane to fly from Oakland to L.A. gives you just enough time to think about a thousand things.

My friend Herb, a friend from grammar school days back in Chi, had graciously offered me some space to crash in for a few months, 'til I reorganized myself.

"Monique ain't here; we got a spare bedroom. Or you can bunk out in the Rumpus Room. It don't matter to me. Whichever one you want."

I looked down onto that dirty, sulphurous cloud that hangs over L.A.

Was it a dream? Had I actually gone to Oakland on the spur of the moment and lived with three beautiful African-American women?

Landing in L.A., I felt as though I was returning to an ugly place. Somehow, I felt as though I had been isolated from the car fumes, the rushing around, the silly behavior of impolite people.

Riding on the assembly line walk, I suddenly felt homesick for the Capoeira Angola classes.

"Themba, I'm going back down to L.A.; know any Capoeira Angola instructors in L.A.?"

"You're going to have to go a lot farther south to find Angola, maybe as far as Brazil."

Kun ba ding da kun ba ding da....

No more Kutiro. It's not something you can learn from a record.

"Moshe, any Kutiro players in L.A. that you know of?"

"I don't know of but four in the United States, and they're here in Oakland."

Tumani, David Frazier, Candido....

Well, I'm sure I'll be able to continue my conga and djimbe lessons.

The sun burst on my eyes like a flashbulb as I walked out of the terminal. Hot and sunny, just the way I like it.

I strolled over to a news vendor, put the coins in, and pulled out a paper.

"Korean grocer kills black teenager."

I stared at the picture of Latasha Harlins, a Black teenager, murdered over a dispute about a container of orange juice.

I felt that I was suddenly pulled back into something I had forgotten about, the African-American/Korean hostilities. I couldn't remember if Oakland had many Korean grocery store owners. In any case, I couldn't recall anyone being murdered over a carton of orange juice.

I stood, waiting for the bus that would start me on the journey to Herb's, remembering the days I had done my personal "survey" of the Black-Korean situation. And the kinds of attitudes I had come across.

The liquor store wars, the mom 'n pop store wars, the Korean/African-American disagreements were escalating.

I pulled my bags on board, puzzled by a couple questions: Why was this the only Asian group that seemed to be having problems with their African-American customers? I couldn't recall anything like this happening with the Chinese restauranteurs (and I've never lived in a Black neighborhood that didn't have a Chinese restaurant; even

204

the worst Chinese restaurant has a chance to succeed), or the Japanese (they might not yell a welcome to the sushi house, but no one pulls a gun out either), and definitely not the Thais, Filipinos, or Vietnamese.

I could feel a novel about the situation brewing in me. I would have to return to the dojang for a bit, to surrender my ego to the discipline before I began asking Master Kim a few questions. It would mean a few months of gruesome physical and emotional suffering, but I felt certain, if anyone had the answers it would definitely be Master Kim. Yeahhh, back to the dojang.

Postscript

Communications. Ife and Kofi ("Friday's child") are talking about having a baby. It's expensive to have her tubes untied, so it's something that they're giving a lot of thought to. When and if the blessed event occurs, I've been asked to be the godfather.

Wodaabe is using her ethnomusicological expertise to assemble a twelve-piece orchestra that uses only natural materials for its music.

Oshun is in Nigeria, visiting her ancestral shrine in Oshogbo. We, all of us, have made a tentative agreement to meet in Kumasi, Ghana, in 1993, for the great drum festival they have there every year.

Master Kim has not, so far, been able to answer any of the questions I've asked him concerning the African-American/Korean problems. Stay tuned.